THE BLUE JAR STORY BOOK

THE BLUE JAR STORY BOOK

**MARIA EDGEWORTH,
CHARLES LAMB,
MARY LAMB,
ALICIA CATHERINE MANT,
ET AL**

ISBN: 978-93-5420-851-5

Published: -

LECTOR HOUSE LLP
E-MAIL: lectorpublishing@gmail.com

"The guinea,—the guinea, sir, that you got from this child!"—Page 16

THE BLUE JAR STORY BOOK

BY

MARIA EDGEWORTH,
CHARLES LAMB,
MARY LAMB,
ALICIA C. MANT AND OTHERS

ILLUSTRATED

CONTENTS

The moment it was on the table Rosamond ran up to it
with an exclamation of joy.

THE BLUE JAR.
MARIA EDGEWORTH.

Rosamond, a little girl about seven years of age, was walking with her mother in the streets of London. As she passed along she looked in at the windows of several shops, and saw a great variety of different sorts of things, of which she did not know the use or even the names. She wished to stop to look at them, but there was a great number of people in the streets, and a great many carts, carriages, and wheelbarrows, and she was afraid to let go her mother's hand.

'Oh, mother, how happy I should be,' she said, as she passed a toy-shop, 'if I had all these pretty things!'

'What, all! Do you wish for them all, Rosamond?'

'Yes, mother, all.'

As she spoke they came to a milliner's shop, the windows of which were decorated with ribands and lace and festoons of artificial flowers.

'Oh mother, what beautiful roses! Won't you buy some of them?'

'No, my dear.'

'Why?'

'Because I don't want them, my dear.'

They went a little farther, and came to another shop, which caught Rosamond's eye. It was a jeweller's shop, and in it were a great many pretty baubles, ranged in drawers behind glass.

'Mother, will you buy some of these?'

'Which of them, Rosamond?'

'Which? I don't know which; any of them will do, for they are all pretty.'

'Yes, they are all pretty; but of what use would they be to me?'

'Use! Oh, I'm sure you could find some use or other for them if you would only buy them first.'

'But I would rather find out the use first.'

'Well, then, mother, there are buckles; you know that buckles are useful things, very useful things.'

'I have a pair of buckles; I don't want another pair,' said her mother, and walked on. Rosamond was very sorry that her mother wanted nothing. Presently, however, they came to a shop which appeared to her far more beautiful than the rest. It was a chemist's shop, but she did not know that.

.'Oh, mother, oh!' cried she, pulling her mother's hand, 'look, look!—blue, green, red, yellow, and purple! Oh, mother, what beautiful things! Won't you buy some of these?'

Still her mother answered as before: 'Of what use would they be to me, Rosamond?'

'You might put flowers in them, mother, and they would look so pretty on the chimney-piece. I wish I had one of them.'

'You have a flower-pot,' said her mother, 'and that is not a flower-pot.'

'But I could use it for a flower-pot, mother, you know.'

'Perhaps, if you were to see it nearer, if you were to examine it, you might be disappointed.'

'No, indeed, I'm sure I should not; I should like it exceedingly.'

Rosamond kept her head turned to look at the blue vase till she could see it no longer.

'Then, mother,' said she, after a pause, 'perhaps you have no money.'

'Yes, I have.'

'Dear me! if I had money I would buy roses, and boxes, and buckles, and blue flower-pots, and everything.' Rosamond was obliged to pause in the midst of her speech. 'Oh, mother, would you stop a minute for me? I have got a stone in my shoe; it hurts me very much.'

'How comes there to be a stone in your shoe?'

'Because of this great hole, mother; it comes in there. My shoes are quite worn out. I wish you would be so very good as to give me another pair.'

'Nay, Rosamond, but I have not money enough to buy shoes, and flower-pots, and buckles, and boxes, and everything.'

Rosamond thought that was a great pity. But now her foot, which had been hurt by the stone, began to give her so much pain that she was obliged to hop every other step, and she could think of nothing else. They came to a shoemaker's shop soon afterwards.

'There, there, mother, there are shoes; there are little shoes that would just fit me, and you know shoes would be really of use to me.'

'Yes, so they would, Rosamond. Come in.' She followed her mother into the shop.

Mr. Sole, the shoemaker, had a great many customers, and his shop was full, so they were obliged to wait.

'Well, Rosamond,' said her mother, 'you don't think this shop so pretty as the rest?'

'No, not nearly; it is black and dark, and there are nothing but shoes all round, and, besides, there's a very disagreeable smell.'

'That smell is the smell of new leather.'

'Is, it? Oh,' said Rosamond looking round 'there is a pair of little shoes; they'll just fit me, I'm sure.'

'Perhaps they might, but you cannot be sure till you have tried them on, any more than you can be quite sure that you should like the blue vase *exceedingly* till you have examined it more attentively.'

'Why, I don't know about the shoes, certainly, till I have tried; but, mother, I am quite sure that I should like the flower-pot.'

'Well, which would you rather have—that jar or a pair of shoes? I will buy either for you.'

'Dear mother, thank you! but if you could buy both?'

'No, not both.'

'Then the jar, if you please.'

'But I should tell you, that in that case I shall not give you another pair of shoes this month.'

'This month! that's a very long time indeed! You can't think how these hurt me. I believe I'd better have the new shoes. Yet, that blue flower-pot. Oh, indeed, mother, these shoes are not so very very bad! I think I might wear them a little longer, and the month will soon be over. I can make them last till the end of the month, can't I? Don't you think so, mother?'

'Nay, my dear, I want you to think for yourself; you will have time enough to consider the matter whilst I speak to Mr. Sole about my clogs.'

Mr. Sole was by this time at leisure, and whilst her mother was speaking to him Rosamond stood in profound meditation, with one shoe on and the other in her hand.

'Well, my dear, have you decided?'

'Mother! yes, I believe I have. If you please, I should like to have the flower-pot; that is, if you won't think me very silly, mother.'

'Why, as to that, I can't promise you, Rosamond; but, when you have to judge for yourself, you should choose what will make you happy, and then it would not signify who thought you silly.'

'Then, mother, if that's all, I'm sure the flower-pot would make me happy,' said she, putting on her old shoe again; 'so I choose the flower-pot.'

'Very well, you shall have it. Clasp your shoe, and come home.'

Rosamond clasped her shoe and ran after her mother. It was not long before the shoe came down at the heel, and many times she was obliged to stop to take the stones out of it, and she often limped with pain; but still the thoughts of the blue flower-pot prevailed, and she persisted in her choice.

When they came to the shop with the large window Rosamond felt much pleasure upon hearing her mother desire the servant who was with them to buy the blue jar, and bring it home. He had other commissions, so he did not return with them. Rosamond as soon as she got in ran to gather all her own flowers, which she kept in a corner of her mother's garden.

'I am afraid they'll be dead before the flower-pot comes, Rosamond,' said her mother to her, as she came in with the flowers in her lap.

'No, indeed, mother; it will come home very soon, I dare say. I shall be very happy putting them into the blue flower-pot.'

'I hope so, my dear.'

The servant was much longer returning home than Rosamond had expected; but at length he came, and brought with him the long-wished-for jar. The moment it was set down upon the table, Rosamond ran up to it with an exclamation of joy. 'I may have it now, mother?'

'Yes, my dear! it is yours.'

Rosamond poured the flowers from her lap upon the carpet, and seized the blue flower-pot.

'Oh, dear mother,' cried she, as soon as she had taken off the top, 'but there's something dark in it which smells very disagreeably. What is it? I didn't want this black stuff.'

'Nor I, my dear.'

'But what shall I do with it, mother?'

'That I cannot tell.'

'It will be of no use to me, mother.'

'That I cannot help.'

'But I must pour it out, and fill the flower-pot with water.'

'As you please, my dear.'

'Will you lend me a bowl to pour it into, mother?'

'That was more than I promised you, my dear, but I will lend you a bowl.'

The bowl was produced, and Rosamond proceeded to empty the blue vase. But she experienced much surprise and disappointment on finding, when it was entirely empty, that it was no longer a *blue* vase. It was a plain white glass jar, which had appeared to have that beautiful colour merely from the liquor with which it had been filled.

Little Rosamond burst into tears.

'Why should you cry, my dear?' said her mother; 'it will be of as much use to you now as ever for a flower-pot.'

'But it won't look so pretty on the chimney-piece. I am sure, if I had known that it was not really blue, I should not have wished to have it so much.'

'But didn't I tell you that you had not examined it, and that perhaps you would be disappointed?'

'And so I am disappointed, indeed. I wish I had believed you at once. Now I had much rather have the shoes, for I shall not be able to walk all this month; even walking home that little way hurt me exceedingly. Mother, I will give you the flower-pot back again, and that blue stuff and all, if you'll only give me the shoes.'

'No, Rosamond; you must abide by your own choice, and now the best thing you can possibly do is to bear your disappointment with good humour.'

'I will bear it as well as I can,' said Rosamond, wiping her eyes; and she began slowly and sorrowfully to fill the vase with flowers.

But Rosamond's disappointment did not end here. Many were the difficulties and distresses into which her imprudent choice brought her before the end of the month. Every day her shoes grew worse and worse, till at last she could neither run, dance, jump, nor walk in them. Whenever Rosamond was called to see anything, she was detained pulling her shoes up at the heels, and was sure to be too late. Whenever her mother was going out to walk, she could not take Rosamond with her, for Rosamond had no soles to her shoes; and at length, on the very last day of the month, it happened that her father proposed to take her, with her brother, to a glasshouse which she had long wished to see. She was very happy; but when she was quite ready, had her hat and gloves on, and was making haste downstairs to her brother and father, who were waiting for her at the hall-door, the shoe dropped off. She put it on again in a great hurry, but as she was going across the hall her father turned round. 'Why are you walking slipshod? no one must walk slipshod with me. Why, Rosamond,' said he, looking at her shoes with disgust, 'I thought that you were always neat. Go; I cannot take you with me.'

Rosamond coloured and retired. 'Oh, mother,' said she, as she took off her hat, 'how I wish that I had chosen the shoes! They would have been of so much more use to me than that jar. However, I am sure—no, not quite sure, but I hope I shall be wiser another time.'

THE BASKET-WOMAN.
MARIA EDGEWORTH.

At the foot of a steep, slippery, white hill, near Dunstable, in Bedfordshire, called Chalk Hill, there is a hut, or rather a hovel, which travellers would scarcely suppose could be inhabited, if they did not see the smoke rising from its peaked roof. An old woman lived in this hovel, many years ago, and with her a little boy and girl, the children of a beggar who died and left these orphans perishing with hunger. They thought themselves very happy when the good old woman first took them into her hut, and bid them warm themselves at her small fire, and gave them a crust of mouldy bread to eat. She had not much to give, but what she had she gave with goodwill. She was very kind to these poor children, and worked hard at her spinning-wheel and at her knitting to support herself and them. She earned money also in another way. She used to follow all the carriages as they went up Chalk Hill, and when the horses stopped to take breath or to rest themselves, she put stones behind the carriage-wheels to prevent them from rolling backwards down the steep, slippery hill.

The little boy and girl loved to stand beside the good-natured old woman's spinning wheel when she was spinning, and to talk to her. At these times she taught them something, which she said she hoped they would remember all their lives. She explained to them what is meant by telling the truth, and what it is to be honest. She taught them to dislike idleness, and to wish that they could be useful.

One evening, as they were standing beside her, the little boy said to her: 'Grandmother'—for that was the name by which she liked that these children should call her—'grandmother, how often you are forced to get up from your spinning-wheel, and to follow the chaises and coaches up that steep hill, to put stones underneath the wheels to hinder them from rolling back! The people who are in the carriages give you a halfpenny or a penny for doing so, don't they?'

'Yes, child.'

'But it is very hard work for you to go up and down that hill. You often say that you are tired. And then you know that you cannot spin all that time. Now, if we might go up the hill, and put the stones behind the wheels, you could sit still at your work; and would not the people give us the halfpence? and could not we bring them all to you? Do, pray, dear grandmother, try us for one day—to-morrow will you?'

'Yes,' said the old woman, 'I will try what you can do; but I must go up the hill along with you for the first two or three times, for fear you should get yourselves hurt.'

So the next day the little boy and girl went with their grandmother, as they used to call her, up the steep hill, and she showed the boy how to prevent the wheels from rolling back by putting stones behind them, and she said: 'This is called scotching the wheels,' and she took off the boy's hat and gave it to the little girl to hold up to the carriage-windows ready for the halfpence.

When she thought that the children knew how to manage by themselves she left them and returned to her spinning-wheel. A great many carriages happened to go by this day, and the little girl received a great many halfpence. She carried them all in her brother's hat to her grandmother in the evening, and the old woman smiled and thanked the children. She said that they had been useful to her, and that her spinning had gone on finely, because she had been able to sit still at her wheel all day.

'But, Paul, my boy,' said she, 'what is the matter with your hand?'

'Only a pinch—only one pinch that I got as I was putting a stone behind a wheel of a chaise. It does not hurt me much, grandmother, and I've thought of a good thing for to-morrow. I shall never be hurt again if you will only be so good as to give me the old handle of the broken crutch, grandmother, and the block of wood that lies in the chimney-corner, and that is of no use. I'll make it of some use, if I may have it.'

'Take it, then, dear,' said the old woman, 'and you'll find the handle of the broken crutch under my bed.'

Paul went to work immediately, and fastened one end of the pole into the block of wood, so as to make something like a dry-rubbing brush.

'Look, grandmother—look at my *scotcher*! I call this thing my *scotcher*,' said Paul, 'because I shall always scotch the wheels with it. I shall never pinch my fingers again; my hands, you see, will be safe at the end of this long stick. And, Sister Anne, you need not be at the trouble of carrying any more stones after me up the hill; we shall never want stones any more. My scotcher will do without anything else, I hope. I wish it was morning, and that a carriage would come, that I might run up the hill and try my scotcher.'

'And I wish that as many chaises may go by to-morrow as there did to-day, and that we may bring you as many halfpence, too, grandmother,' said the little girl.

'So do I, my dear Anne,' said the old woman, 'for I mean that you and your brother shall have all the money that you get to-morrow. You may buy some gingerbread for yourselves, or some of those ripe plums that you saw at the fruit-stall the other day, which is just going into Dunstable. I told you then that I could not afford to buy such things for you, but now that you can earn halfpence for yourselves, children, it is fair you should taste a ripe plum and bit of gingerbread for once and a way in your lives.'

'We'll bring some of the gingerbread home to her, shan't we, brother?' whispered little Anne.

"Look, grandmother—look at my scotcher!"

The morning came, but no carriages were heard though Paul and his sister had risen at five o'clock that they might be sure to be ready for early travellers. Paul kept his scotcher poised upon his shoulder, and watched eagerly at his station at the bottom of the hill. He did not wait long before a carriage came. He followed it up the hill, and the instant the postillion called to him and bade him stop the wheels, he put his scotcher behind them, and found that it answered the purpose perfectly well.

Many carriages went by this day, and Paul and Anne received a great many halfpence from the travellers.

When it grew dusk in the evening Anne said to her brother: 'I don't think any more carriages will come by to-day. Let us count the halfpence, and carry them home now to grandmother.'

'No, not yet,' answered Paul; 'let them alone—let them lie still in the hole where I have put them. I dare say more carriages will come by before it is quite dark, and then we shall have more halfpence.'

Paul had taken the halfpence out of his hat, and he had put them into a hole in the high bank by the roadside, and Anne said she would not meddle with them, and that she would wait till her brother liked to count them; and Paul said: 'If you will stay and watch here, I will go and gather some blackberries for you in the hedge in yonder field. Stand you hereabouts, half-way up the hill, and the moment you see any carriage coming along the road run as fast as you can and call me.'

Anne waited a long time, or what she thought a long time, and she saw no carriage and she trailed her brother's scotcher up and down till she was tired. Then she stood still and looked again, and she saw no carriage, so she went sorrowfully into the field and to the hedge where her brother was gathering blackberries, and she said:

'Paul, I'm sadly tired—*sadly tired!*' said she, 'and my eyes are quite strained with looking for chaises. No more chaises will come to-night, and your scotcher is lying there, of no use, upon the ground. Have not I waited long enough for to-day, Paul?'

'Oh no,' said Paul. 'Here are some blackberries for you; you had better wait a little bit longer. Perhaps a carriage might go by whilst you are standing here talking to me.'

Anne, who was of a very obliging temper, and who liked to do what she was asked to do, went back to the place where the scotcher lay, and scarcely had she reached the spot when she heard the noise of a carriage. She ran to call her brother, and, to their great joy, they now saw four chaises coming towards them. Paul, as soon as they went up the hill, followed with his scotcher. First he scotched the wheels of one carriage, then of another; and Anne was so much delighted with observing how well the scotcher stopped the wheels, and how much better it was than stones, that she forgot to go and hold her brother's hat to the travellers for halfpence, till she was roused by the voice of a little rosy girl who was looking out of the window of one of the chaises. 'Come close to the chaise-door,' said the little girl; 'here are some halfpence for you.'

Anne held the hat, and she afterwards went on to the other carriages. Money was thrown to her from each of them, and when they had all gotten safely to the top of the hill, she and her brother sat down upon a large stone by the roadside to count their treasure. First they began by counting what was in the hat—'One, two, three, four halfpence.'

'But, oh, brother, look at this!' exclaimed Anne; 'this is not the same as the other halfpence.'

'No, indeed, it is not,' cried Paul; 'it is no halfpenny. It is a guinea—a bright golden guinea!'

'Is it?' said Anne, who had never seen a guinea in her life before, and who did not know its value, 'and will it do as well as a halfpenny to buy gingerbread? I'll run to the fruit-stall and ask the woman, shall I?'

'No, no,' said Paul, 'you need not ask any woman, or anybody but me. I can tell you all about it as well as anybody in the whole world.'

'The whole world! Oh, Paul, you forgot. Not so well as my grandmother.'

'Why, not so well as my grandmother, perhaps; but, Anne, I can tell you that you must not talk yourself, Anne, but you must listen to me quietly, or else you won't understand what I am going to tell you; for I can assure you that I don't think I quite understood it myself, Anne, the first time my grandmother told it to me, though I stood stock-still listening my best.'

Prepared by this speech to hear something very difficult to be understood, Anne looked very grave, and her brother explained to her that with a guinea she might buy two hundred and fifty-two times as many plums as she could get for a penny.

'Why, Paul, you know the fruit-woman said she would give us a dozen plums for a penny. Now, for this little guinea would she give us two hundred and fifty-two dozen?'

'If she has so many, and if we like to have so many, to be sure she will,' said Paul; 'but I think we should not like to have two hundred and fifty-two dozen of plums; we could not eat such a number.'

'But we could give some of them to my grandmother,' said Anne.

'But still there would be too many for her, and for us, too,' said Paul, 'and when we had eaten the plums there would be an end to all the pleasure. But now I'll tell you what I am thinking of, Anne, that we might buy something for my grandmother that would be very useful to her indeed with the guinea—something that would last a great while.'

'What, brother? What sort of thing?'

'Something that she said she wanted very much last winter, when she was so ill with the rheumatism—something that she said yesterday, when you were making her bed, she wished she might be able to buy before next winter.'

"We might buy something very useful with the guinea."

'I know, I know what you mean!' said Anne—'a blanket. Oh, yes, Paul, that will be much better than plums; do let us buy a blanket for her. How glad she will be to see it! I will make her bed with the new blanket, and then bring her to look at it. But, Paul, how shall we buy a blanket? Where are blankets to be got?'

'Leave that to me; I'll manage that. I know where blankets can be got; I saw one hanging out of a shop the day I went last to Dunstable.'

'You have seen a great many things at Dunstable, brother.'

'Yes, a great many; but I never saw anything there or anywhere else that I wished for half so much as I did for the blanket for my grandmother. Do you remember how she used to shiver with the cold last winter? I'll buy the blanket to-morrow. I'm going to Dunstable with her spinning.'

'And you'll bring the blanket to me, and I shall make the bed very neatly. That will be all right—all happy!' said Anne, clapping her hands.

'But stay! Hush! don't clap your hands so, Anne. It will not be all happy, I'm afraid,' said Paul, and his countenance changed, and he looked very grave. 'It will not be all right, I'm afraid, for there's one thing we have neither of us thought of, but that we ought to think about. We cannot buy the blanket, I'm afraid.'

'Why—Paul, why?'

'Because I don't think this guinea is honestly ours.'

'Nay, brother, but I'm sure it is honestly ours. It was given to us, and grandmother said all that was given to us to-day was to be our own.'

'But who gave it to you, Anne?'

'Some of the people in those chaises, Paul. I don't know which of them, but I dare say it was the little rosy girl.'

'No,' said Paul, 'for when she called you to the chaise door she said, "Here's some halfpence for you." Now, if she gave you the guinea, she must have given it to you by mistake.'

'Well, but perhaps some of the people in the other chaises gave it to me, and did not give it to me by mistake, Paul. There was a gentleman reading in one of the chaises, and a lady, who looked very good-naturedly at me, and then the gentleman put down his book, and put his head out of the window and looked at your scotcher, brother, and he asked me if that was your own making; and when I said yes, and that I was your sister, he smiled at me, and put his hand into his waistcoat pocket, and threw a handful of halfpence into the hat, and I dare say he gave us the guinea along with them because he liked your scotcher so much.'

'Why,' said Paul, 'that might be, to be sure, but I wish I was quite certain of it.'

'Then, as we are not quite certain, had not we best go and ask my grandmother what she thinks about it?'

Paul thought this was excellent advice, and he was not a silly boy who did not like to follow good advice. He went with his sister directly to his grandmother, showed her the guinea and told her how they came by it.

'My dear honest children,' said she, 'I am very glad you told me all this. I am very glad that you did not buy either the plums or the blanket with this guinea. I'm sure it is not honestly ours. Those who threw it you gave it you by mistake, I warrant, and what I would have you do is to go to Dunstable, and try if you can at either of the inns find out the person who gave it to you. It is now so late in the evening that perhaps the travellers will sleep at Dunstable instead of going on the next stage; and it is likely that whosoever gave you a guinea instead of a halfpenny has found out their mistake by this time. All you can do is to go and inquire for the gentleman who was reading in the chaise.'

'Oh!' interrupted Paul, 'I know a good way of finding him out. I remember it was a dark-green chaise with red wheels, and I remember I read the innkeeper's name upon the chaise, "John Nelson." (I am much obliged to you for teaching me to read, grandmother.) You told me yesterday, grandmother, that the names written upon chaises are the innkeepers to whom they belong. I read the name of the innkeeper upon that chaise. It was John Nelson. So Anne and I will go to both the inns in Dunstable, and try to find out this chaise—John Nelson's. Come, Anne, let us set out before it gets quite dark.'

Anne and her brother passed with great courage the tempting stall that was covered with gingerbread and ripe plums, and pursued their way steadily through the streets of Dunstable; but Paul, when he came to the shop where he had seen the blanket, stopped for a moment, and said: 'It is a great pity, Anne, that the guinea is not ours. However, we are doing what is honest, and that is a comfort. Here, we must go through this gateway into the inn-yard; we are come to the Dun Cow.'

'Cow!' said Anne, 'I see no cow.'

'Look up, and you'll see the cow over your head,' said Paul—'the sign, the picture. Come, never mind looking at it now; I want to find out the green chaise that has John Nelson's name upon it.'

Paul pushed forward through a crowded passage till he got into the inn-yard. There was a great noise and bustle. The ostlers were carrying in luggage; the postillions were rubbing down the horses, or rolling the chaises into the coach-house.

'What now? What business have you here, pray?' said a waiter, who almost ran over Paul as he was crossing the yard in a great hurry to get some empty bottles from the bottle-rack. 'You've no business here, crowding up the yard. Walk off, young gentleman, if you please.'

'Pray give me leave, sir,' said Paul, 'to stay a few minutes to look amongst these chaises for one dark-green chaise with red wheels that has Mr. John Nelson's name written upon it.'

'What's that he says about a dark-green chaise?' said one of the postillions.

'What should such a one as he is know about chaises?' interrupted the hasty waiter, and he was going to turn Paul out of the yard; but the ostler caught hold of his arm, and said: 'Maybe the child *has* some business here; let's know what he has to say for himself.'

The waiter was at this instant luckily obliged to leave them to attend the bell, and Paul told his business to the ostler, who as soon as he saw the guinea and heard the story shook Paul by the hand, and said: 'Stand steady, my honest lad. I'll find the chaise for you, if it is to be found here; but John Nelson's chaises almost always drive to the Black Bull.'

After some difficulty the green chaise with John Nelson's name upon it, and the postillion who drove that chaise, were found, and the postillion told Paul that he was just going into the parlour to the gentleman he had driven to be paid, and that he would carry the guinea with him.

'No,' said Paul; 'we should like to give it back ourselves.'

'Yes,' said the ostler, 'that they have a right to do.'

The postillion made no reply, but looked vexed, and went on towards the house, desiring the children would wait in the passage till his return. In the passage there was standing a decent, clean, good-natured looking woman with two huge straw baskets on each side of her. One of the baskets stood a little in the way of the entrance. A man who was pushing his way in, and carried in his hand a string of dead larks hung to a pole, impatient at being stopped, kicked down the straw basket, and all its contents were thrown out. Bright straw hats, and boxes, and slippers, were all thrown in disorder upon the dirty ground.

'Oh, they will be trampled upon! They will all be spoiled!' exclaimed the woman to whom they belonged.

'We'll help you to pick them up, if you will let us,' cried Paul and Anne, and they immediately ran to her assistance.

When the things were all safe in the basket again the children expressed a desire to know how such beautiful things could be made of straw, but the woman had not time to answer before the postillion came out of the parlour, and with him a gentleman's servant, who came to Paul, and clapping him upon the back, said:

'So, my little chap, I gave you a guinea for a halfpenny, I hear, and I understand you've brought it back again; that's right, give me hold of it.'

'No, brother,' said Anne, 'this is not the gentleman that was reading.'

'Pooh, child! I came in Mr. Nelson's green chaise. Here's the postillion can tell you so. I and my master came in that chaise. I and my master that was reading, as you say, and it was he that threw the money out to you. He is going to bed; he is tired, and can't see you himself. He desires that you'll give me the guinea.'

Paul was too honest himself to suspect that this man was telling him a falsehood, and he now readily produced his bright guinea, and delivered it into the servant's hands.

'Here's a sixpence apiece for you, children,' said he, 'and good-night to you.' He pushed them towards the door, but the basket-woman whispered to them as they went out: 'Wait in the street till I come to you.'

'Pray, Mrs. Landlady,' cried this gentleman's servant, addressing himself to the landlady, who just then came out of a room where some company at supper—'pray, Mrs. Landlady, please to let me have roasted larks for my supper. You are famous for larks at Dunstable, and I make it a rule to taste the best of everything wherever I go; and, waiter, let me have a bottle of claret. Do you hear?'

'Larks and claret for his supper,' said the basket-woman to herself as she looked at him from head to foot. The postillion was still waiting, as if to speak to him, and she observed them afterwards whispering and laughing together. '*No bad hit,*' was a sentence which the servant pronounced several times.

Now, it occurred to the basket-woman that this man had cheated the children out of the guinea to pay for the larks and claret, and she thought that perhaps she could discover the truth. She waited quietly in the passage.

'Waiter! Joe! Joe!' cried the landlady, 'why don't you carry in the sweet-meat-puffs and the tarts here to the company in the best parlour?'

'Coming, ma'am,' answered the waiter, and with a large dish of tarts and puffs he came from the bar. The landlady threw open the door of the best parlour to let him in, and the basket-woman had now a full view of a large cheerful company, and amongst them several children, sitting round a supper-table.

'Ay,' whispered the landlady, as the door closed after the waiter and the tarts, 'there are customers enough, I warrant, for you in that room, if you had but the luck to be called in. Pray, what would you have the conscience, I wonder now, to charge me for these here half-dozen little mats to put under my dishes?'

'A trifle, ma'am,' said the basket-woman. She let the landlady have the mats cheap, and the landlady then declared she would step in and see if the company in the best parlour had done supper. 'When they come to their wine,' added she, 'I'll speak a good word for you, and get you called in afore the children are sent to bed.'

The landlady, after the usual speech of '*I hope the supper and everything is to your liking, ladies and gentlemen,*' began with: 'If any of the young gentlemen or ladies would have a *cur'osity* to see any of our famous Dunstable straw-work there's a decent body without would, I dare say, be proud to show them her pincush-ion-boxes, and her baskets and slippers, and her other *cur'osities.*'

The eyes of the children all turned towards their mother; their mother smiled, and immediately their father called in the basket-woman, and desired her to pro-duce her *curiosities*. The children gathered round her large pannier as it opened, but they did not touch any of her things.

'Ah, papa,' cried a little rosy girl, 'here are a pair of straw slippers that would just fit you, I think; but would not straw shoes wear out very soon, and would not they let in the wet?'

'Yes, my dear,' said her father, 'but these slippers are meant—'

'For powdering-slippers, miss,' interrupted the basket-woman.

'To wear when people are powdering their hair,' continued the gentleman, 'that they may not spoil their other shoes.'

'And will you buy them, papa?'

'No, I cannot indulge myself,' said her father, 'in buying them now. I must make amends,' said he, laughing, 'for my carelessness, and as I threw away a guin-ea to-day I must endeavour to save sixpence at least.'

'Ah, the guinea that you threw by mistake into the little girl's hat as we were coming up Chalk Hill. Mamma, I wonder that the little girl did not take notice of its being a guinea, and that she did not run after the chaise to give it back again. I should think, if she had been an honest girl, she would have returned it.'

'Miss!—ma'am!—sir!' said the basket-woman, 'if it would not be impertinent, may I speak a word? A little boy and girl have just been here inquiring for a gentleman who gave them a guinea instead of a halfpenny by mistake and not five minutes ago I saw the boy give the guinea to a gentleman's servant, who is there without, and who said his master desired it should be returned to him.'

'There must be some mistake or some trick in this,' said the gentleman. 'Are the children gone? I must see them; send after them.'

'I'll go for them myself,' said the good-natured basket-woman. 'I bid them wait in the street yonder, for my mind misgave me that the man who spoke so short to them was a cheat, with his larks and his claret.'

Paul and Anne were speedily summoned, and brought back by their friend the basket-woman; and Anne, the moment she saw the gentleman, knew that he was the very person who smiled upon her, who admired her brother's scotcher, and who threw a handful of halfpence into the hat; but she could not be certain, she said, that she received the guinea from him: she only thought it most likely that she did.

'But I can be certain whether the guinea you returned be mine or no,' said the gentleman. 'I marked the guinea; it was a light one, the only guinea I had, which I put into my waistcoat pocket this morning.' He rang the bell, and desired the waiter to let the gentleman who was in the room opposite to him know that he wished to see him.

'The gentleman in the white parlour, sir, do you mean?'

'I mean the master of the servant who received a guinea from this child.'

'He is a Mr. Pembroke, sir,' said the waiter.

Mr. Pembroke came, and as soon as he heard what had happened he desired the waiter to show him to the room where his servant was at supper. The dishonest servant who was supping upon larks and claret, knew nothing of what was going on; but his knife and fork dropped from his hand, and he overturned a bumper of claret as he started up from the table in great surprise and terror, when his master came in with a face of indignation, and demanded, '*The guinea—the guinea, sir,* that you got from this child! that guinea which you said I ordered you to ask for from this child!'

The servant, confounded and half intoxicated, could only stammer out that he had more guineas than one about him, and that he really did not know which it was. He pulled his money out, and spread it upon the table with trembling hands. The marked guinea appeared. His master instantly turned him out of his service, with strong expressions of contempt.

'And now, my little honest girl,' said the gentleman who had admired her brother's scotcher, turning to Anne—'and now tell me who you are, and what you and your brother want or wish for most in the world.'

In the same moment Anne and Paul exclaimed: 'The thing we wish for the most in the world is a blanket for our grandmother.'

'She is not our grandmother in reality, I believe sir,' said Paul; 'but she is just as good to us, and taught me to read, and taught Anne to knit, and taught us both that we should be honest—so she has, and I wish she had a new blanket before next winter to keep her from the cold and the rheumatism. She had the rheumatism sadly last winter, sir, and there is a blanket in this street that would be just the thing for her.'

'She shall have it, then; and,' continued the gentleman, 'I will do something more for you. Do you like to be employed or to be idle best?'

'We like to have something to do always, if we could, sir,' said Paul; 'but we are forced to be idle sometimes, because grandmother has not always things for us to do that we *can* do well.'

'Should you like to learn how to make such baskets as these?' said the gentleman, pointing to one of the Dunstable straw baskets.

'Oh, very much!' said Paul.

'Very much!' said Anne.

'Then I should like to teach you how to make them,' said the basket-woman, 'for I'm sure of one thing, that you'd behave honestly to me.'

The gentleman put a guinea into the good natured basket-woman's hand, and told her that he knew she could not afford to teach them her trade for nothing. 'I shall come through Dunstable again in a few months,' added he, 'and I hope to see that you and your scholars are going on well. If I find that they are I will do something more for you.'

'But,' said Anne, 'we must tell all this to grandmother, and ask her about it; and I'm afraid—though I'm very happy—that it is getting very late, and that we should not stay here any longer.'

'It is a fine moonlight night,' said the basket-woman, 'and is not far. I'll walk with you, and see you safe home myself.'

The gentleman detained them a few minutes longer, till a messenger whom he had despatched to purchase the much-wished-for blanket returned.

'Your grandmother will sleep well upon this good blanket, I hope,' said the gentleman, as he gave it into Paul's opened arms. 'It has been obtained for her by the honesty of her adopted children.'

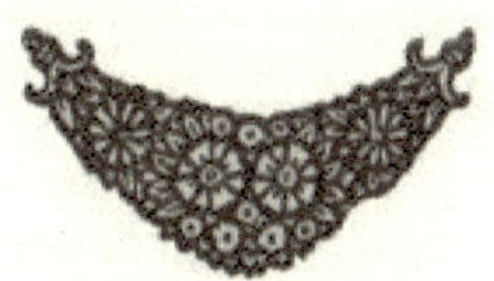

THE SEA VOYAGE.
CHARLES LAMB.

I was born in the East Indies. I lost my father and mother young. At the age of five my relations thought it proper that I should be sent to England for my education. I was to be entrusted to the care of a young woman who had a character for great humanity and discretion; but just as I had taken leave of my friends, and we were about to take our passage, the young woman suddenly fell sick, and could not go on board. In this unpleasant emergency, no one knew how to act. The ship was at the very point of sailing, and it was the last which was to sail for the season. At length the captain, who was known to my friends, prevailed upon my relation who had come with us to see us embark to leave the young woman on shore, and to let me embark separately. There was no possibility of getting any other female attendant for me in the short time allotted for our preparation, and the opportunity of going by that ship was thought too valuable to be lost. No other ladies happened to be going, and so I was consigned to the care of the captain and his crew—rough and unaccustomed attendants for a young creature, delicately brought up as I had been; but, indeed, they did their best to make me not feel the difference. The unpolished sailors were my nursery-maids and my waiting-women. Everything was done by the captain and the men to accommodate me and make me easy. I had a little room made out of the cabin, which was to be considered as my room, and nobody might enter into it. The first mate made a great character for bravery, and all sailor-like accomplishments; but with all this he had a gentleness of manners, and a pale, feminine cast of face, from ill-health and a weakly constitution, which subjected him to some ridicule from the officers, and caused him to be named Betsy. He did not much like the appellation, but he submitted to it the better, saying that those who gave him a woman's name well knew that he had a man's heart, and that in the face of danger he would go as far as any man. To this young man, whose real name was Charles Atkinson, by a lucky thought of the captain the care of me was especially entrusted. Betsy was proud of his charge, and, to do him justice, acquitted himself with great diligence and adroitness through the whole of the voyage. From the beginning I had somehow looked upon Betsy as a woman, hearing him so spoken of, and this reconciled me in some measure to the want of a maid, which I had been used to. But I was a manageable girl at all times, and gave nobody much trouble.

I have not knowledge enough to give an account of my voyage, or to remember the names of the seas we passed through or the lands which we touched upon in our course. The chief thing I can remember (for I do not recollect the events of the voyage in any order) was Atkinson taking me upon deck to see the great whales playing about the sea. There was one great whale came bounding up out of the sea, and then he would dive into it again, and then he would come up at a distance where nobody expected him, and another whale was following after him. Atkinson said they were at play, and that the lesser whale loved that bigger whale, and kept it company all through the wide seas; but I thought it strange play and a frightful kind of love, for I every minute expected they would come up to our ship and toss it. But Atkinson said a whale was a gentle creature, and it was a sort of sea-elephant, and that the most powerful creatures in Nature are always the least hurtful. And he told me how men went out to take these whales, and stuck long pointed darts into them; and how the sea was discoloured with the blood of these poor whales for many miles' distance; and I admired the courage of the men, but I was sorry for the inoffensive whale. Many other pretty sights he used to show me, when he was not on watch or doing some duty for the ship. No one was more attentive to his duty than he, but at such times as he had leisure he would show me all pretty sea-sights: the dolphins and porpoises that came before a storm, and all the colours which the sea changed to—how sometimes it was a deep blue, and then a deep green, and sometimes it would seem all on fire. All these various appearances he would show me, and attempt to explain the reason of them to me, as well as my young capacity would admit of. There were a lion and a tiger on board going to England as a present to the King, and it was a great diversion to Atkinson and me, after I had got rid of my first terrors, to see the ways of these beasts in their dens, and how venturous the sailors were in putting their hands through the grates, and patting their rough coats. Some of the men had monkeys, which ran loose about, and the sport was for the men to lose them, and find them again. The monkeys would run up the shrouds and pass from rope to rope, with ten times greater alacrity than the most experienced sailor could follow them, and sometimes they would hide themselves in the most unthought-of places, and when they were found, they would grin and make mouths, as if they had sense. Atkinson described to me the ways of these little animals in their native woods, for he had seen them. Oh, how many ways he thought of to amuse me in that long voyage!

Sometimes he would describe to me the odd shapes and varieties of fishes that were in the sea, and tell me tales of the sea-monsters that lay hid at the bottom, and were seldom seen by men, and what a glorious sight it would be if our eyes could be sharpened to behold all the inhabitants of the sea at once, swimming in the great deeps, as plain as we see the gold and silver fish in a bowl of glass. With such notions he enlarged my infant capacity to take in many things.

When in foul weather I have been terrified at the motion of the vessel, as it rocked backwards and forwards, he would still my fears, and tell me that I used to be rocked so once in a cradle, and that the sea was God's bed and the ship our cradle, and we were as safe in that great motion as when we felt that lesser one in our little wooden sleeping-places. When the wind was up, and sang through the sails, and disturbed me with its violent clamours, he would call it music, and bid me hark to the sea-organ, and with that name he quieted my tender apprehensions. When I have looked around with a mournful face at seeing all *men* about me, he would enter into my thoughts, and tell me pretty stories of his mother and his sisters, and a female cousin that he loved better than his sisters, whom he called Jenny, and say that when we got to England I should go and see them, and how fond Jenny would be of his little daughter, as he called me; and with these images of women and females which he raised in my fancy he quieted me for a while. One time, and never but once he told me that Jenny had promised to be his wife if ever he came to England, but that he had his doubts whether he should live to get home, for he was very sickly. This made me cry bitterly.

"He would show me all pretty sea-sights."

That I dwell so long upon the attention of this Atkinson is only because his death, which happened just before we got to England, affected me so much, that he alone of all the ship's crew has engrossed my mind ever since, though, indeed, the captain and all were singularly kind to me, and strove to make up for my uneasy and unnatural situation. The boatswain would pipe for my diversion, and the sailor-boy would climb the dangerous mast for my sport. The rough fore-mast-man would never willingly appear before me till he had combed his long black hair smooth and sleek, not to terrify me. The officers got up a sort of play for my amusement, and Atkinson, or, as they called him, Betsy, acted the heroine of the piece. All ways that could be contrived were thought upon to reconcile me to my lot. I was the universal favourite. I do not know how deservedly, but I suppose it was because I was alone, and there was no female in the ship besides me. Had I come over with female relations or attendants, I should have excited no particular curiosity, I should have required no uncommon attentions. I was one little woman among a crew of men, and I believe the homage which I have read that men universally pay to women was in this case directed to me, in the absence of all other womankind. I do not know how that might be, but I was a little princess among them, and I was not six years old.

I remember the first drawback which happened to my comfort was Atkinson's not appearing the whole of one day. The captain tried to reconcile me to it by saying that Mr. Atkinson was confined to his cabin, that he was not quite well, but a day or two would restore him. I begged to be taken in to see him, but this was not granted. A day, and then another came, and another, and no Atkinson was visible, and I saw apparent solicitude in the faces of all the officers, who nevertheless strove to put on their best countenances before me, and to be more than usually kind to me. At length, by the desire of Atkinson himself, as I have since learned, I was permitted to go into his cabin and see him. He was sitting up, apparently in a state of great exhaustion; but his face lighted up when he saw me, and he kissed me, and told me that he was going a great voyage, far longer than that which we had passed together, and he should never come back; and though I was so young, I understood well enough that he meant this of his death, and I cried sadly; but he comforted me, and told me that I must be his little executrix, and perform his last will, and bear his last words to his mother and his sisters, and to his cousin Jenny, whom I should see in a short time, and he gave me his blessing, as a father would bless his child, and he sent a last kiss by me to all his female relations, and he made me promise that I would go and see them when I got to England, and soon after this he died. But I was in another part of the ship when he died, and I was not told it till we got to shore, which was a few days after. But they kept telling me that he was better and better, and that I should soon see him, but that it disturbed him to talk with anyone. Oh, what a grief it was when I learned that I had lost an old shipmate, that had made an irksome situation so bearable by his kind assiduities, and to think that he was gone, and I could never repay him for his kindness!

When I had been a year and a half in England, the captain, who had made another voyage to India and back, thinking that time alleviated a little the sorrow of Atkinson's relations, prevailed upon my friends who had the care of me in England to let him introduce me to Atkinson's mother and sisters. Jenny was no more; she had died in the interval, and I never saw her. Grief for his death had brought on a consumption, of which she lingered about a twelvemonth, and then expired. But in the mother and the sisters of this excellent young man I have found the most valuable friends I possess on this side the great ocean. They received me from the captain as the little protége of Atkinson, and from them I have learned passages of his former life, and this in particular—that the illness of which he died was brought on by a wound of which he never quite recovered which he got in the desperate attempt, when he was quite a boy, to defend his captain against a superior force of the enemy which had boarded him, and which, by his premature valour, inspiriting the men, they finally succeeded in repulsing. This was that Atkinson who, from his pale and feminine appearance, was called Betsy. This was he whose womanly care of me got him the name of a woman, who, with more than female attention, condescended to play the handmaid to a little unaccompanied orphan that fortune had cast upon the care of a rough sea-captain and his rougher crew.

THE CHANGELING.

MARY LAMB.

My name, you know, is Withers; but as I once thought I was the daughter of Sir Edward and Lady Harriet Lesley, I shall speak of myself as Miss Lesley, and call Sir Edward and Lady Harriet my father and mother during the period I supposed them entitled to those beloved names. When I was a little girl, it was the perpetual subject of my contemplation that I was an heiress, and the daughter of a baronet; that my mother was the Honourable Lady Harriet; that we had a nobler mansion, infinitely finer pleasure-grounds, and equipages more splendid than any of the neighbouring families. I am ashamed to confess what a proud child I once was. How it happened I cannot tell, for my father was esteemed the best-bred man in the country, and the condescension and affability of my mother were universally spoken of.

Alas! I am a changeling, substituted by my mother for the heiress of the Lesley family. It was for my sake she did this naughty deed; yet, since the truth has been known, it seems to me as if I had been the only sufferer by it; remembering no time when I was not Harriet Lesley, it seems as if the change had taken from me my birthright.

Lady Harriet had intended to nurse her child herself, but being seized with a violent fever soon after its birth, she was not only unable to nurse it but even to see it, for several weeks. I was not quite a month old at this time when my mother was hired to be Miss Lesley's nurse. She had once been a servant in the family; her husband was then at sea.

She had been nursing Miss Lesley a few days, when a girl who had the care of me brought me into the nursery to see my mother. It happened that she wanted something from her own home, which she despatched the girl to fetch, and desired her to leave me till her return. In her absence she changed our clothes; then, keeping me to personate the child she was nursing, she sent away the daughter of Sir Edward to be brought up in her own poor cottage.

When my mother sent away the girl, she affirmed she had not the least intention of committing this bad action; but after she was left alone with us, she looked on me, and then on the little lady baby, and she wept over me, to think she was obliged to leave me to the charge of a careless girl, debarred from my own natural food, while she was nursing another person's child.

The laced cap and the fine cambric robe of the little Harriet were lying on the table ready to be put on. In these she dressed me, only just to see how pretty her own dear baby would look in missy's fine clothes. When she saw me thus adorned, she said to me:

"The girl carried her away without the least suspicion
that it was not the same infant."

'Oh, my dear Ann, you look as like missy as anything can be! I am sure my lady herself, if she were well enough to see you, would not know the difference!'

She said these words aloud, and while she was speaking a wicked thought came into her head—how easy it would be to change these children! On which she hastily dressed Harriet in my coarse raiment. She had no sooner finished the transformation of Miss Lesley into the poor Ann Withers than the girl returned, and carried her away, without the least suspicion that it was not the same infant that she had brought thither.

It was wonderful that no one discovered that I was not the same child. Every fresh face that came into the room filled the nurse with terror. The servants still continued to pay their compliments to the baby in the same form as usual, crying:

'How like it is to its father!'

Nor did Sir Edward himself perceive the difference, his lady's illness probably engrossing all his attention at the time, though, indeed, gentlemen seldom take much notice of very young children.

When Lady Harriet began to recover, and the nurse saw me in her arms caressed as her own child, all fears of detection were over; but the pangs of remorse then seized her. As the dear sick lady hung with tears of fondness over me, she thought she should have died with sorrow for having so cruelly deceived her.

When I was a year old, Mrs. Withers was discharged, and because she had been observed to nurse me with uncommon care and affection, and was seen to shed many tears at parting from me, to reward her fidelity Sir Edward settled a small pension on her, and she was allowed to come every Sunday to dine in the housekeeper's room, and see her little lady.

When she went home, it might have been expected she would have neglected the child she had so wickedly stolen, instead of which she nursed it with the greatest tenderness, being very sorry for what she had done. All the ease she could ever find for her troubled conscience was in her extreme care of this injured child, and in the weekly visits to its father's house she constantly brought it with her. At the time I have the earliest recollection of her she was become a widow, and with the pension Sir Edward allowed her, and some plain work she did for our family, she maintained herself and her supposed daughter. The doting fondness she showed for her child was much talked of. It was said she waited upon it more like a servant than a mother, and it was observed its clothes were always made, as far as her slender means would permit, in the same fashion, and her hair cut and curled in the same form, as mine. To this person, as having been my faithful nurse, and to her child, I was always taught to show particular civility, and the little girl was always brought into the nursery to play with me. Ann was a little delicate thing, and remarkably well behaved, for, though so much indulged in every other respect, my mother was very attentive to her manners.

As the child grew older my mother became very uneasy about her education. She was so very desirous of having her well behaved that she feared to send her to school, lest she should learn ill manners among the village children, with whom she never suffered her to play, and she was such a poor scholar herself that she could teach her little or nothing. I heard her relate this her distress to my own maid, with tears in her eyes, and I formed a resolution to beg of my parents that I might have Ann for a companion, and that she might be allowed to take lessons with me of my governess.

My birthday was then approaching, and on that day I was always indulged in the privilege of asking some peculiar favour.

'And what boon has my annual petitioner to beg to-day?' said my father, as he entered the breakfast-room on the morning of my birthday.

Then I told him of the great anxiety expressed by Nurse Withers concerning her daughter; how much she wished it was in her power to give her an education that would enable her to get her living without hard labour. I set the good qualities of Ann Withers in the best light I could, and in conclusion I begged she might be permitted to partake with me in education, and become my companion.

'This is a very serious request indeed, Harriet,' said Sir Edward. 'Your mother and I must consult together on the subject.'

The result of this conversation was favourable to my wishes. In a few weeks my foster-sister was taken into the house, and placed under the tuition of my governess.

To me, who had hitherto lived without any companions of my own age, except occasional visitors, the idea of a play-fellow constantly to associate with was very pleasant, and, after the first shyness of feeling her altered situation was over, Ann seemed as much at her ease as if she had always been brought up in our house. I became very fond of her, and took pleasure in showing her all manner of attentions, which so far won on her affections that she told me she had a secret entrusted to her by her mother, which she had promised never to reveal as long as her mother lived, but that she almost wished to confide it to me, because I was such a kind friend to her; yet, having promised never to tell it till the death of her mother, she was afraid to tell it to me. At first I assured her that I would never press her to the disclosure, for that promises of secrecy were to be held sacred; but whenever we fell into any confidential kind of conversation, this secret seemed always ready to come out. Whether she or I were most to blame, I know not, though I own I could not help giving frequently hints how well I could keep a secret. At length she told me what I have before related—namely, that she was in truth the daughter of Sir Edward and Lady Lesley, and I the child of her supposed mother.

When I was first in possession of this wonderful secret, my heart burned to reveal it. I thought how praiseworthy it would be in me to restore to my friend the rights of her birth; yet I thought only of becoming her patroness, and raising her to her proper rank. It never occurred to me that my own degradation must necessarily follow. I endeavoured to persuade her to let me tell this important affair to my parents. This she positively refused. I expressed wonder that she should so faithfully keep this secret for an unworthy woman, who in her infancy had done her such an injury.

'Oh,' said she, 'you do not know how much she loves me, or you would not wonder that I never resent that. I have seen her grieve and be so very sorry on my account that I would not bring her into more trouble for any good that could happen to myself. She has often told me that, since the day she changed us, she has never known what it is to have a happy moment, and when she returned home from nursing you, finding me very thin and sickly, how her heart smote her for what she had done; and then she nursed and fed me with such anxious care that she grew much fonder of me than if I had been her own, and that on the Sundays when she used to bring me here it was more pleasure to her to see me in my father's own house than it was to her to see you, her real child. The shyness you showed towards her while you were very young, and the forced civility you seemed to affect as you grew older, always appeared like ingratitude towards her who had done so much for you. My mother has desired me to disclose this after her death, but I do not believe I shall ever mention it then, for I should be sorry to bring any reproach even on her memory.'

In a short time after this important discovery, Ann was sent home to pass a few weeks with her mother, on the occasion of the unexpected arrival of some visitors to our house. They were to bring children with them, and these I was to consider as my own guests.

In the expected arrival of my young visitants, and in making preparations to entertain them, I had little leisure to deliberate on what conduct I should pursue with regard to my friend's secret. Something must be done, I thought, to make her amends for the injury she had sustained, and I resolved to consider the matter attentively on her return. Still my mind ran on conferring favours. I never considered myself as transformed into the dependent person. Indeed, Sir Edward at this time set me about a task which occupied the whole of my attention. He proposed that I should write a little interlude, after the manner of the French 'Petites Pièces,' and to try my ingenuity, no one was to see it before the representation, except the performers, myself, and my little friends, who, as they were all younger than I, could not be expected to lend me much assistance. I have already told you what a proud girl I was. During the writing of this piece, the receiving of my young friends, and the instructing them in their several parts, I never felt myself of so much importance. With Ann my pride had somewhat slumbered. The difference of our rank left no room for competition; all was complacency and good-humour on my part, and affectionate gratitude, tempered with respect, on hers. But here I had full room to show courtesy, to affect those graces, to imitate that elegance of manners, practised by Lady Harriet to their mothers. I was to be their instructress in action and in attitudes, and to receive their praises and their admiration of my theatrical genius. It was a new scene of triumph for me, and I might then be said to be in the very height of my glory.

If the plot of my piece, for the invention of which they so highly praised me, had been indeed my own, all would have been well; but unhappily I borrowed from a source which made my drama end far differently from what I intended it should. In the catastrophe I lost not only the name I personated in the piece, but with it my own name also, and all my rank and consequence in the world fled from me for ever. My father presented me with a beautiful writing-desk for the use of my new authorship. My silver standish was placed upon it; a quire of gilt paper was before me. I took out a parcel of my best crow quills, and down I sate in the greatest form imaginable.

"Many sheets were scrawled over in vain. I could think of nothing else."

I conjecture I have no talent for invention. Certain it is that, when I sat down to compose my piece, no story would come into my head but the story which Ann had so lately related to me. Many sheets were scrawled over in vain; I could think of nothing else. Still the babies and the nurse were before me in all the minutiæ of description Ann had given them. The costly attire of the lady baby, the homely garb of the cottage infant, the affecting address of the fond mother to her own off-spring, then the charming *équivoque* in the change of the children—it all looked so dramatic. It was a play ready-made to my hands. The invalid mother would form the pathetic, the silly exclamations of the servants the ludicrous, and the nurse was nature itself. It is true I had a few scruples that it might, should it come to the knowledge of Ann, be construed into something very like a breach of confidence. But she was at home, and might never happen to hear of the subject of my piece, and if she did, why, it was only making some handsome apology. To a dependent companion to whom I had been so very great a friend, it was not necessary to be so very particular about such a trifle.

Thus I reasoned as I wrote my drama, beginning with the title, which I called 'The Changeling,' and ending with these words: 'The curtain drops, while the lady clasps the baby in her arms, and the nurse sighs audibly.' I invented no new incident; I simply wrote the story as Ann had told it to me, in the best blank verse I was able to compose.

By the time it was finished the company had arrived. The casting the different parts was my next care. The Honourable Augustus M——, a young gentleman of five years of age, undertook to play the father. He was only to come in and say: 'How does my little darling do to-day?' The three Miss —— s were to be the servants; they, too, had only single lines to speak.

As these four were all very young performers, we made them rehearse many times over, that they might walk in and out with proper decorum; but the performance was stopped before their entrances and their exits arrived. I complimented Lady Elizabeth, the sister of Augustus, who was the eldest of the young ladies, with the choice of the lady mother, or the nurse. She fixed on the former. She was to recline on a sofa, and, affecting ill-health, speak some eight or ten lines, which began with, 'Oh, that I could my precious baby see!' To their cousin, Miss Emily ----, was given the girl who had the care of the nurse's child. Two dolls were to personate the two children, and the principal character of the nurse I had the pleasure to perform myself. It consisted of several speeches, and a very long soliloquy during the changing of the children's clothes.

The elder brother of Augustus, a gentleman of fifteen years of age, refused to mix in our childish drama, yet condescended to paint the scenes, and our dresses were got up by my own maid.

When we thought ourselves quite perfect in our several parts, we announced it for representation. Sir Edward and Lady Harriet, with their visitors, the parents of my young troop of comedians, honoured us with their presence. The servants were also permitted to go into a music-gallery, which was at the end of a ball-room we had chosen for our theatre.

As author and principal performer, standing before a noble audience, my mind was too much engaged with the arduous task I had undertaken to glance my eyes towards the music-gallery, or I might have seen two more spectators there than I expected. Nurse Withers and her daughter Ann were there; they had been invited by the housekeeper to be present at the representation of Miss Lesley's play.

In the midst of the performance, as I, in character of the nurse, was delivering the wrong child to the girl, there was an exclamation from the music-gallery of:

'Oh, it's all true! it's all true!'

This was followed by a bustle among the servants, and screams as of a person in an hysteric fit. Sir Edward came forward to inquire what was the matter. He saw it was Mrs. Withers who had fallen into a fit. Ann was weeping over her, and crying out:

'Oh, Miss Lesley, you have told all in the play!'

Mrs. Withers was brought out into the ball-room. There, with tears and in broken accents, with every sign of terror and remorse, she soon made a full confession of her so long-concealed guilt.

The strangers assembled to see our childish mimicry of passion were witnesses to a highly-wrought dramatic scene in real life. I intended that they should see the curtain drop without any discovery of the deceit. Unable to invent any new incident, I left the conclusion imperfect as I found it. But they saw a more strict poetical justice done; they saw the rightful child restored to its parents, and the nurse overwhelmed with shame, and threatened with the severest punishment.

'Take this woman,' said Sir Edward, 'and lock her up till she be delivered into the hands of justice.'

Ann, on her knees, implored mercy for her mother. Addressing the children, who were gathered round her, 'Dear ladies,' said she, 'help me—on your knees help me—to beg forgiveness for my mother!' Down the young ones all dropped; even Lady Elizabeth bent on her knee. 'Sir Edward, pity her distress! Sir Edward pardon her!'

All joined in the petition except one, whose voice ought to have been loudest in the appeal. No word, no accent came from me. I hung over Lady Harriet's chair, weeping as if my heart would break. But I wept for my own fallen fortunes, not for my mother's sorrow.

I thought within myself: 'If in the integrity of my heart, refusing to participate in this unjust secret, I had boldly ventured to publish the truth, I might have had some consolation in the praises which so generous an action would have merited; but it is through the vanity of being supposed to have written a pretty story that I have meanly broken my faith with my friend, and unintentionally proclaimed the disgrace of my mother and myself.'

While thoughts like these were passing through my mind, Ann had obtained my mother's pardon. Instead of being sent away to confinement and the horrors of a prison, she was given by Sir Edward into the care of the housekeeper, who had orders from Lady Harriet to see her put to bed and properly attended to, for again this wretched woman had fallen into a fit.

Ann would have followed my mother, but Sir Edward brought her back, telling her that she should see her when she was better. He then led her towards Lady Harriet, desiring her to embrace her child. She did so, and I saw her, as I had phrased it in the play, 'clasped in her mother's arms.'

This scene had greatly affected the spirits of Lady Harriet. Through the whole of it, it was with difficulty she had been kept from fainting, and she was now led into the drawing-room by the ladies. The gentlemen followed, talking with Sir Edward of the astonishing instance of filial affection they had just seen in the earnest pleadings of the child for her supposed mother.

Ann, too, went with them, and was conducted by her whom I had always considered as my own particular friend. Lady Elizabeth took hold of her hand, and said:

'Miss Lesley, will you permit me to conduct you to the drawing-room?'

I was left weeping behind the chair where Lady Harriet had sate, and, as I thought, quite alone. A something had before twitched my frock two or three times, so slightly I had scarcely noticed it. A little head now peeped round, and looking up in my face, said:

'She is not Miss Lesley!'

It was the young Augustus. He had been sitting at my feet, but I had not observed him. He then started up, and taking hold of my hand with one of his, with the other holding fast by my clothes, he led, or rather dragged, me into the midst of the company assembled in the drawing-room. The vehemence of his manner, his little face as red as fire, caught every eye. The ladies smiled, and one gentleman laughed in a most unfeeling manner. His elder brother patted him on the head, and said:

'You are a humane little fellow. Elizabeth, we might have thought of this.'

Very kind words were now spoken to me by Sir Edward, and he called me Harriet, precious name now grown to me. Lady Harriet kissed me, and said she would never forget how long she had loved me as her child. These were comfortable words, but I heard echoed round the room:

'Poor thing! *she* cannot help it! I am sure *she* is to be pitied! Dear Lady Harriet, how kind, how considerate you are!'

Ah! what a deep sense of my altered condition did I then feel!

'Let the young ladies divert themselves in another room,' said Sir Edward; 'and Harriet, take your new sister with you, and help her to entertain your friends.'

Yes, he called me Harriet again, and afterwards invented new names for his daughter and me, and always called us by them, apparently in jest; yet I knew it was only because he would not hurt me with hearing our names reversed. When Sir Edward desired us to show the children into another room, Ann and I walked towards the door. A new sense of humiliation arose. How could I go out at the door before Miss Lesley? I stood irresolute. She drew back. The elder brother of my friend Augustus assisted me in this perplexity. Pushing us all forward, as if in a playful mood, he drove us indiscriminately before him, saying:

'I will make one among you to-day.'

He had never joined in our sports before.

My luckless play, that sad instance of my duplicity, was never once mentioned to me afterwards, not even by any one of the children who had acted in it, and I must also tell you how considerate an old lady was at the time about our dresses. As soon as she perceived things growing very serious, she hastily stripped off the upper garments we wore to represent our different characters. I think I should have died with shame if the child had led me into the drawing-room in the mummery I had worn to represent a nurse. This good lady was of another essential service to me, for, perceiving an irresolution in everyone how they should behave to us, which distressed me very much, she contrived to place Miss Lesley above me at table, and called her Miss Lesley, and me Miss Withers, saying at the same time in a low voice, but as if she meant I should hear her,

'It is better these things should be done at once, then they are over.'

My heart thanked her, for I felt the truth of what she said.

My poor mother continued very ill for many weeks. No medicine could remove the extreme dejection of spirits she laboured under. Sir Edward sent for Dr. Wheelding, the clergyman of the parish, to give her religious consolation. Every day he came to visit her, and he would always take Miss Lesley and me into the room with him.

My heart was softened by my own misfortunes, and the sight of my penitent, suffering mother. I felt that she was now my only parent. I strove, earnestly strove, to love her; yet ever when I looked in her face, she would seem to me to be the very identical person whom I should have once thought sufficiently honoured by a slight inclination of the head, and a civil, 'How do you do, Mrs Withers?' One day, as Miss Lesley was hanging over her with her accustomed fondness, Dr. Wheelding reading in a Prayer-Book, and, as I thought, not at that moment regarding us, I threw myself on my knees, and silently prayed that I, too, might be able to love my mother.

Dr. Wheelding had been observing me. He took me into the garden, and drew from me the subject of my petition.

'Your prayers, my good young lady,' said he, 'I hope, are heard. Sure I am they have caused me to adopt a resolution which, as it will enable you to see your mother frequently, will, I hope, greatly assist your pious wishes. I will take your mother home with me to superintend my family. Under my roof doubtless Sir Edward will often permit you to see her. Perform your duty towards her as well as you possibly can. Affection is the growth of time. With such good wishes in your young heart, do not despair that in due time it will assuredly spring up.'

With the approbation of Sir Edward and Lady Harriet, my mother was removed in a few days to Dr. Wheelding's house. There she soon recovered! there she at present resides. She tells me she loves me almost as well as she did when I was a baby, and we both wept at parting when I went to school.

THE INQUISITIVE GIRL.

ANON.

Dr. Hammond was a physician in great practice in the West of England. He resided in a small market-town, and his family consisted of one son named Charles, and two daughters, Louisa and Sophy.

Sophy possessed many amiable qualities, and did not want for sense, but every better feeling was lost in her extreme inquisitiveness. Her faculties were all occupied in peeping and prying about, and, provided she could gratify her own curiosity, she never cared how much vexation she caused to others.

This propensity began when she was so very young that it had become a habit before her parents perceived it. She was a very little creature when she was once nearly squeezed to death between two double doors as she was peeping through the keyhole of one of them to see who was in the drawing-room; and another time she was locked up for several hours in a closet in which she had hid herself for the purpose of overhearing what her mother was saying to one of the servants.

When Sophy was eleven and her sister about sixteen years old their mother died. Louisa was placed at the head of her father's house, and the superintendence of Sophy's education necessarily devolved on her. The care of such a family was a great charge for a young person of Miss Hammond's age, and more especially as her father was obliged to be so much from home that she could not always have his counsel and advice even when she most needed it. By this means she fell into an injudicious mode of treating her sister.

If Louisa received a note she carefully locked it up, and never spoke of its contents before Sophy. If a message was brought to her she always went out of the room to receive it, and never suffered the servant to speak in her sister's hearing. When any visitors came Louisa commonly sent Sophy out of the room, or if they were intimate friends she would converse with them in whispers; in short, it was her chief study that everything which passed in the family should be a secret from Sophy. Alas! this procedure, instead of repressing Sophy's curiosity, only made it the more keen; her eyes and ears were always on the alert, and what she could not see, hear, or thoroughly comprehend she made out by guesses.

The worst consequence of Louisa's conduct was that as Sophy had no friend and companion in her sister, who treated her with such constant suspicion and reserve, she necessarily was induced to find a friend and companion amongst the servants, and she selected the housemaid Sally, a good-natured, well-intentioned girl, but silly and ignorant and inquisitive like herself, and it may be easily supposed how much mischief these two foolish creatures occasioned, not only in the family, but also amongst their neighbours.

If Louisa received a note she carefully locked it up.

It happened soon after that, for an offence which was the cause of very great vexation to her brother, and was the occasion of his being for a time deprived of the friendship of Sir Henry and Lady Askham, two of Dr. Hammond's nearest and most intimate neighbours, her father ordered Sophy, as a still further punishment, to be locked up in her own room till the Sunday following. This was on Friday, and Sophy had two days of solitude and imprisonment before her. The first day she passed very dismally, but yet not unprofitably, for she felt truly ashamed and sorry for her fault, and made many good resolutions of endeavouring to cure herself of her mischievous propensity. The second day she began to be somewhat more composed, and by degrees she was able to amuse herself with watching the people in the street, which was overlooked by the windows of her apartment, and she began, almost unconsciously to herself, to indulge in her old habit of trying to find out what everybody was doing, and in guessing where they were going.

She had not long been engaged in watching her neighbours before her curiosity was excited by the appearance of a servant on horseback, who rode up to the door, and, after giving a little three-cornered note to Dr. Hammond's footman, rode off. The servant she knew to be Mrs. Arden's, an intimate friend of her father, and the note she conjectured was an invitation to dinner, and the guessing what day the invitation was for, and who were to be the company, and whether she was included in the invitation, was occupying her busy fancy, when she saw her sister going out of the house with the three-cornered note in her hand, and cross the street to Mr. McNeal's stocking shop, which was opposite. Almost immediately afterwards Mr. McNeal's shopman came out of the shop, and, running down the street, was presently out of sight, but soon returned with Mr. McNeal himself. She saw Louisa reading the note to Mr. McNeal, and in a few minutes afterwards returned home. Here was matter of wonder and conjecture. Sophy forgot all her good resolutions, and absolutely wearied herself with her useless curiosity.

At length the term of her imprisonment was over, and Sophy was restored to the society of her family. At first she kept a tolerable guard over herself. Once she saw her father and sister whispering, and did not, though she longed much to do it, hold her breath that she might hear what they were saying. Another time she passed Charles's door when it was ajar and the little study open, and she had so much self-command that she passed by without peeping in, and she began to think she was cured of her faults. But in reality this was far from being the case, and whenever she recollected Mrs. Arden's mysterious note she felt her inquisitive propensities as strong as ever. Her eyes and ears were always on the alert, in hopes of obtaining some clue to the knowledge she coveted, and if Mrs. Arden's or Mr. McNeal's names were mentioned she listened with trembling anxiety in the hope of hearing some allusion to the note.

At last, when she had almost given up the matter in despair, an unlooked-for chance put her in possession of a fragment of this very note to which she attached so much importance.

One day Louisa wanted to wind a skein of silk, and in looking for a piece of paper to wind it upon she opened her writing-box, and took out Mrs. Arden's note. Sophy knew it again in an instant from its three-cornered shape. She saw her sister tear the note in two, throw one-half under the grate, and fold the other part up to wind her silk upon. Sophy kept her eye on the paper that lay under the grate in the greatest anxiety, lest a coal should drop upon it and destroy it, when it seemed almost within her grasp. Louisa was called out of the room, and Sophy, overpowered by the greatness of the temptation, forgot all the good resolutions she had so lately made, and at the risk of setting fire to her sleeve, snatched the paper from amongst the ashes, and concealed it in her pocket. She then flew to her own room to examine it at her case. The note had been torn lengthway of the paper, and that part of it of which Sophy had possessed herself contained the first half of each line of the note. Bolting her door for fear of interruption, she read, with trembling impatience, as follows:

'Will you
be kind enough to go to
Mr. McNeal, and tell him
he has made a great mistake
the last stockings he sent;
(charging them as silk) he has cheated
of several pounds.—I am sorry to say
that he has behaved very ill
And Mr. Arden tells me that
it must end in his being hanged
I am exceedingly grieved
but fear this will be the end.'

When Sophy had read these broken sentences she fancied that she fully comprehended the purport of the whole note, and she now saw the reason of her sister's hastening to Mr. McNeal's immediately on the receipt of the note, and of the hurry in which he had been summoned back to his shop. It appeared very clear to her that he had defrauded Mrs. Arden of a considerable sum of money, and that he was no longer that honest tradesman he had been supposed. The weight of this important discovery quite overburdened her, and, forgetful of her past punishment, and regardless of future consequences, she imparted the surprising secret to Sally. Sally was not one who could keep such a piece of news to herself; it was therefore soon circulated through half the town that Mr. McNeal had defrauded Mrs. Arden, and that Mr. Arden declared he would have him hanged for it. Several persons in consequence avoided Mr. McNeal's shop, who saw his customers forsaking him without being able to know why they did so. Thus the conduct of this inconsiderate girl took away the good name of an honest tradesman, on no better foundation than her own idle conjectures drawn from the torn fragments of a letter.

Mr. McNeal at length became informed of the injurious report that was circulated about him. He immediately went to Mrs. Arden to tell her of the report, and to ask her if any inadvertency of his own in regard to her dealings at his shop had occasioned her speaking so disadvantageously of him. Mrs. Arden was much astonished at what he told her, as she might well be, and assured him that she had never either spoken of him nor thought of him but as thoroughly an honourable and honest tradesman. Mrs. Arden was exceedingly hurt that her name should be attached to such a cruel calumny, and, on consulting with Sir Henry Askham, it was agreed that he and Mrs. Arden should make it their business to trace it back to its authors. They found no great difficulty in tracing it back to Sally, Dr. Hammond's servant. She was accordingly sent for to Mr. McNeal's, where Sir Henry Askham and Mr. Arden, with some other gentlemen, were assembled on this charitable investigation. Sally, on being questioned who had told her of the report replied, without hesitation, that she had been told by Miss Sophy, who had seen all the particulars in Mrs. Arden's handwriting.

She read it with trembling impatience.

Mr. Arden was greatly astonished at hearing this assertion, and felt confident that the whole must have originated from some strange blunder. He and the other gentlemen immediately proceeded to Dr. Hammond's, and having explained their business to him, desired to see Sophy. She, on being asked, confirmed what Sally had said, adding that to satisfy them she could show them Mrs. Arden's own words, and she accordingly produced the fragment of the note. Miss Hammond, the instant she saw the paper recollected it again, and winding off the silk from the other half of Mrs. Arden's note, presented it to Mr. Arden, who, laying the two pieces of paper together, read as follows:

'MY DEAR MISS HAMMOND,—Will you as soon as you receive this be kind enough to go to your opposite neighbour, Mr. Mc-Neal, and tell him I find by looking at his bill he has made a great mistake as to the price of the last stockings he sent; and it seems to me (by not charging them as silk) he has cheated himself, as he'll see, of several pounds.—I am sorry to say of our new dog, that he has behaved very ill and worried two sheep, and Mr. Arden tells me that he very much fears it must end in his being hanged or he'll kill all the flock. I am exceedingly grieved, for he is a noble animal, but fear this will be the end of my poor dog. 'I am, dear Louisa, yours truly,

'MARY ARDEN.'

Thus by the fortunate preservation of the last half of the note the whole affair was cleared up, Mrs. Arden's character vindicated from the charge of being a defamer, and Mr. McNeal from all suspicion of dishonesty. And all their friends were pleased and satisfied. But how did Sophy feel? She did feel at last both remorse and humiliation. She had no one to blame but herself; she had no one to take her part, for even her father and her brother considered it due to public justice that she should make a public acknowledgment of her fault to Mr. McNeal, and to ask his pardon.

THE LITTLE BLUE BAG.

ALICIA CATHERINE MANT.

'I think,' said Agnes Clavering, a child of about eight years of age—'I think I should like to give that pretty blue bag I admired so much the other day at the Bazaar to my cousin Laura. She likes blue, and I know she wishes for a new bag.'

'You will do very well, Agnes, in thus spending a part of your allowance of pocket-money,' replied Mrs. Clavering. 'Laura is one of the kindest little girls I know, and, being one of a large family, cannot have so many indulgences as yourself; and I am always glad when I see you bear this in mind.'

'I shall give it her on New Year's Day,' continued Agnes, after a few minutes of thoughtfulness, 'for it was on that day of this year that she gave me that pretty purse of her own making; and I shall buy a gold thimble to put in it, and a pretty little pair of scissors with a gold sheath, and a tortoiseshell box for needles, and some ivory winders for cotton.'

'All these together,' replied Mrs. Clavering, 'will make a very handsome present, and I am sure that Laura will be much pleased with it. But do you know how long it is to New Year's Day?'

'No, mother; I do not,' replied Agnes.

'Nearly six weeks,' said Mrs. Clavering; 'but you may make your purchases the first time we walk through the Bazaar, and then you will have them ready against the time you require them.'

Nothing more passed at that time on the subject of the blue bag, and that and several following days being wet, there was no opportunity of visiting the Bazaar. During this time Mrs. Clavering and Agnes went to dine with Mr. and Mrs. Parker, and when Agnes, on going to play with her cousins after dinner, saw Laura's shabby workbasket, and heard her complain of having broken her needle and hurt her finger by a hole in her thimble, Agnes felt very glad that she had happened to recollect what Laura wanted. She could hardly help telling her what was in preparation for her. More than once it was on the very tip of her tongue, and the secret certainly would have been revealed had not little Augusta Parker suddenly fallen against a table, which stood in the corner of the play-room and thrown its contents on the floor.

'Oh, Augusta!' said Laura, in a tone of vexation; but she checked herself, and helping the little girl to rise, kindly asked her if she had hurt herself.

The child, however, was unhurt, and knowing that Laura would be vexed at the upset she had occasioned, she crept to the other end of the room, and began playing with her little brothers.

'Oh, what beautiful shells!' said Agnes. 'Where did you get them, and why did you not show them to me, Laura? I am so fond of shells!' For it was a box of shells which the little Augusta had thrown off the table.

'I did not mean you to see them yet,' replied Laura—'not till the box was full; but it does not signify now,' added the placid little girl; and the two children sat down together to examine this little mine of treasures.

Agnes was not at all envious of Laura's box of shells, but Agnes would very much have liked to have had a box with shells placed in them exactly as Laura's were. It was one of her failings to wish to have the same toy or the same trinket which she saw in the possession of other little girls. It was not her desire to deprive them of theirs, but she wished to possess something exactly similar, and it had been her misfortune from the moment of her being able to form any wishes to have them immediately gratified. The consequence was that she was whimsical and capricious. The favourite wax doll of to-day would be discarded on the morrow for one of wood if she saw one of that sort in the hands of another. Her playthings never pleased her more than two or three days, and at the end of this time a string of new desires arose, which she knew would be immediately met, and which consequently led the way to others. She had only to ask and have, and this facility gradually produced a sort of selfishness which her mother was vexed at perceiving. Agnes was kind-hearted, and always willing that others should be gratified, but not at her expense; and Mrs. Clavering saw that, while any little present the child made to her friends, or charity bestowed on some poor object, occasioned no deprivation to herself, the motives for both could not be pure.

When she had reached her eighth year, therefore, early as it might seem, Mrs. Clavering had set aside a purse for the use of her little girl, which she told her was all that would be expended for her amusements during the year, and she was anxious to see how far this arrangement might be a check on the boundless wishes of the little Agnes. Hitherto Agnes had gone on very well. Her father's presents, in spite of her mother's remonstrances, had kept the purse nearly full, and at the latter end of January it would be again replenished. But her father was now from home. It might so happen that he would be absent till that time, and Agnes knew that she must now use her means with caution.

As she was returning with her mother home in the carriage from her uncle's, Agnes said:

'I should so very much like a box of shells.'

'And have you not as much pleasure in looking at Laura's?' replied Mrs. Clavering. 'And do you not think she has some pleasure in showing you what you have not of your own? It is very seldom indeed that she can have this pleasure, for you have everything, and a great deal more than she has. It so happens in this case that her father's brother has given her what I think it would be hardly in the power of your father to buy, for he brought them from abroad. And I hope you will be satisfied to see them when you are with your cousin, and be very careful of expressing any wish for them before her. For you know that she has more than once offered you such little trifles as you have wished for when you have seen them in her possession.'

'Oh, mother,' said Agnes, with eagerness, 'I do not want Laura's shells, indeed! I only wanted some like them. But I will try and not think of the shells.'

'You should not do this, Agnes,' said Mrs. Clavering; 'you should try and think of them without wishing for them. But here we are at home.'

A few days after this a lady called on Mrs. Clavering to invite her to go with her to look at some old china, and Agnes received permission to be of the party. While the two ladies were occupied with the master of the shop in looking through his assortment of china, the master's wife very good-naturedly busied herself with Agnes, and endeavoured to amuse her by showing her many curiosities contained on her numerous shelves. Amongst the rest she exhibited some drawers of shells, some of which were so like those which Agnes had seen in Laura's box that she began to long for them, and as the prices were marked, and they did not appear very expensive, she whispered to her mother and asked if she might purchase them.

'Can you afford it?' whispered Mrs. Clavering in reply, and stroking at the same time the blooming cheek that rested against hers.

'I think I can, mother,' again whispered Agnes, in a very coaxing manner.

'If you are *sure* you can,' once more whispered Mrs. Clavering, 'you may; but remember the blue bag.'

Agnes returned to the tempting shell-drawer. Mrs. Clavering advanced the money to pay for the new purchases, and on their return home Agnes begged her mother would directly pay herself from her own purse.

'And, mother,' continued Agnes, 'I think the thimble shall be of silver instead of gold, for a gold one will cost a great deal of money. And I never use a gold one, and why should I give Laura one?'

'I see no reason why, certainly,' answered Mrs. Clavering, 'excepting that it was your own proposal. I should have thought that a silver one was quite as well, if not better; but I did not like to check your wish of making a handsome present to your cousin. Let it be silver, if you please; but take care that you keep money enough to pay for that, and the other articles which you design putting into the New Year's present.'

'Oh, I shall have plenty now, mother,' returned Agnes; 'but I think I could not have afforded the gold thimble.'

And she went to her play-room to look at her shells, put them in order, and see how many were wanting to complete the number which her cousin possessed.

It now occurred to her that a box to contain them was indispensable, and the footman's brother being a carpenter, she desired him to get one made for her. It was soon completed, and when it came home, and was paid for, Agnes found that it had cost just the difference between a silver and a gold thimble. She proceeded to place her shells in order, but the box was not half full, and while thus occupied a visitor called, who was accompanied by her young son and a beautiful little white dog, and this little white dog and his master called off her attention for a while from her shells.

The little animal was very amusing and very playful. He could perform a number of little odd tricks, and, amongst others, would patiently wait while his young master counted ten, and then would spring forwards and receive the piece of bread or biscuit held out to him. Agnes thought she never could be tired of playing with such a 'dear little dog,' to use her own expression, and she expressed her wishes so strongly and so earnestly that the little dog's master, after whispering to his mother, told Agnes that if she liked she was very welcome to keep the dog, for that he was going to school, and nobody at home cared for her but himself. Mrs. Clavering felt vexed that Agnes had so warmly expressed her admiration of the dog, but she did not see how she could decline her acceptance, and by this arrangement Agnes for the remainder of the day had nothing to wish for, excepting, indeed, it might be that the chapter of the History of England she read to her mother in the evening had not been quite so long, and that bedtime had not come before she had had another game of play with little Chloe.

In the morning the first thing to be thought of was Chloe, and Chloe occasioned in her mistress so many wandering thoughts when she ought to have been occupied with her book that Mrs. Clavering was obliged to threaten the loss of the new favourite before the morning task could be accomplished. At length Chloe was turned out of the room, but then Chloe would run downstairs, and into the hall, and back again upstairs, and scratch at the drawing-room door for admittance, and when once more admitted, on Agnes's promise to let her lie still quietly under the sofa, Chloe wished to go out of the room again; and out of the room once more, but only once, she was allowed to go. Then, on the hall-door being left open for a minute, Chloe was out in the street, and it was with considerable difficulty that James, the man-servant, could again catch her. This suggested the necessity of a collar for Chloe, and a collar, indeed, seemed indispensable if the dog was to be kept.

'But I am not sure that I shall have money enough to buy one,' said Agnes, as she begged her mother to examine her purse, and assist her in calculating how much the blue bag and its furniture were likely to cost.

Agnes thought, if father was at home she would have had the collar purchased for her directly, and as Mrs. Clavering had allowed the dog to be accepted, it seemed to her that it would not be an unreasonable indulgence to make Chloe's mistress a present of a collar. She told Agnes, therefore, that she would provide the little animal with a collar, and thinking that the sooner the blue bag was bought the less would be Agnes's temptation to encroach on the money set aside for its purchase, she directed her little girl to get her hat and pelisse put on, and they would proceed immediately to the Bazaar.

As Mrs. Clavering and Agnes were crossing the hall, a carriage drove to the door. It was Mrs. Montague, a particular friend of Mrs. Clavering, and she had called to invite her and Agnes to take a drive to a bird-fancier's, who had a large collection of canary-birds; for Harriet and Eliza Montague had been promised by their uncle that they should each have one, and their mother thought that Agnes would like to go and help choose them. The little girls had a very pleasant ride together, and they all thought the birds very beautiful, and that they sung delightfully. But it was rather an unfortunate excursion for Agnes, for on her return home Chloe pleased her no longer, and she told her mother she thought 'a canary-bird would be a much prettier pet than a rude, troublesome little dog.'

'And yet you were very much pleased with your little dog yesterday,' remarked Mrs. Clavering, 'and to-day she looks much prettier with her smart collar on, and she frisks and gambols about, and is as anxious as ever to be taken notice of.'

At this moment Chloe ran up to her little mistress, and Agnes could not help acknowledging that her collar was very pretty. She kissed her mother for having so soon obliged her by buying one, and for an hour or two the canary-birds were forgotten. The next day, however, Agnes had been invited to spend with Harriet and Eliza Montague. The birds had been brought home. They looked even more beautiful in the play-room than at the bird-fancier's, and they and their cages together were so very ornamental that Agnes thought of them some minutes after she had laid her head on her pillow. In the morning she asked her mother if she might not buy a canary-bird. They were not very expensive, and she should like one so very much.'

'I wish my dear little girl, you could learn to see what others have, and be amused and pleased, without always wishing to possess what has given you amusement and pleasure.'

'If I can but have a canary-bird,' replied Agnes, 'I shall not wish for anything else, and shall be quite satisfied. Do, mother, let me buy one. Father would, I know, if he were at home.'

'Your father is very indulgent, Agnes,' replied Mrs. Clavering. 'He sees you but seldom, and never likes to refuse you anything you wish for when he does see you; but I should not think you a good girl to impose upon his kindness by asking anything of him which I had thought it better to refuse you.'

'I cannot see why I should not have a canary-bird, mother,' said Agnes, not, I am sorry to say, very good-humouredly, 'and I do not wish you to buy it for me. I could buy it myself, for, you know, I have money of my own.'

'I do not mean to argue with you,' replied Mrs. Clavering, 'for little girls of your age are not always capable of understanding the reason why indulgences are refused them, though they are quite equal to knowing that it is their duty not to repine when they are withheld. However, do as you please about the canary-bird. If you have money sufficient to pay for one, let the bird be bought. The money was given you to spend exactly as you please.'

Agnes looked at her mother. No, mother did not look pleased—she looked grave; and when Agnes's countenance once more brightened at the prospect of possessing the canary-bird, Mrs. Clavering neither smiled nor even looked at Agnes. She continued looking at her work, and her needle went in and out very, very fast. Agnes walked up to her mother, and taking her purse from the box where it was always kept, took from it the money, and began to count it.

Presently Mrs. Clavering said:

'Well, Agnes, what is this beautiful bird to cost?'

'Only five shillings,' replied Agnes.

'And have you five shillings to spare?' said Mrs. Clavering.

'Oh yes, mother; I think I have,' replied Agnes. 'Oh yes, I can do it very well. You know I talked of buying a gold scissor-sheath for Laura, but I think a leather one will do just as well. And then I shall have more than money enough for the canary-bird.'

'Poor Laura!' said Mrs. Clavering. 'I am afraid she does not stand a very good chance of having any New Year's gift. However, the money is your own, and you are to do what you please with it. But if you did think of others a little more, and less of yourself, Agnes, you would be a much more amiable little girl.'

Agnes for a minute looked grave, for she saw a tear in her mother's eye. But her mother did not look angry, and she went on with her calculations and schemes about canary-birds and cages. James was commissioned to purchase the bird so much desired, and as it was positively necessary that the bird, when bought, should have a habitation to live in, the tortoiseshell box designed for Laura was to be changed into a card needle-case, and the next morning Agnes's play-room was adorned with a very pretty canary-bird in a smart wire cage.

The next day Laura and Augusta Parker came to visit their cousin, but they did not seem to take so much pleasure in the new purchase as it was supposed they would. They were very willing to assist Agnes in feeding her bird, and admired its plumage, which they thought very pretty and very soft, and they expressed no desire to be playing with anything else, for they saw Agnes was better pleased to be taking down and putting up her cage than in following any other amusement. But they would much rather have been playing with Agnes's new doll, or looking at some of her story-books, or puzzles, or play-things, of which she had such useless stores; and when she did lead them to some of these, neither Laura nor Augusta thought more of the canary-bird, except when it sang so loudly as to prevent the little girls from hearing each other speak. Indeed, it did sing so loudly that nothing else could be heard, and Agnes herself was at length so tired of it that she was sorry it had been purchased. Her dear cousin Laura, too, who was so gentle and good-natured, had lost part of her pretty present by the purchase of this useless bird, and she should be ashamed to tell her mother she was tired of it.

But she did not allow these thoughts to make her miserable, and the three little girls spent a very happy as well as a very busy day, for Laura set all Agnes's cupboards and drawers to rights for her, and looked over her maps and puzzles, and placed the right pieces in the right boxes; and she sewed in some leaves that were torn out of some of the prettiest story-books, for Agnes was very careless with her books, and she placed them all in nice even rows upon the shelves. Then she mended the doll's frock, and made a very pretty new doll's bonnet; and Augusta made a tippet, all herself, even the cutting out and fitting, though she was only six years old; and she set the doll's house in order, and wiped the dust from off the little chairs and tables; and, in short, nothing could be so happy and comfortable as were the three little girls together. Then at last they came to the box with the shells, but this Agnes preferred not looking at, for she had very few shells, compared to her cousin's collection, and the box was not half so pretty, for Laura's box was inlaid with ivory; and as Augusta was seizing upon the shells with her little dusting-cloth in her hand, Agnes said:

'Oh, leave those, Augusta; they are not worth thinking about.'

'But I thought you were very fond of shells,' said Laura.

'Yes, so I am,' replied Agnes; 'but not such a set as these. They are nothing to yours.' And she turned from them with contempt, and drew Augusta to the other end of the room. 'Come, Augusta, we will play at mother and children. I will be your mother, and Laura and you shall be my children.'

Laura and Augusta instantly agreed to what their cousin proposed, and for some time the play went on smoothly enough. But well inclined as was Augusta to do everything to make herself pleasant and agreeable, she did not like to 'pretend to be naughty' so often as her little mother required of her; and Agnes, as little mothers, I believe, frequently are, was very fond of having her play-child to punish, and set in the corner, and to lecture and scold. Laura thought there was a little too much disgrace, and that she had much rather have been allowed to be good; but Laura never consulted her own wishes in opposition to her playfellows. Besides, Laura was a great girl and could not be supposed to care about these things. But poor Augusta was a very little child and had been accustomed to a great deal of indulgence from Laura, and she began to feel very serious at being so frequently reproved and disgraced. She really thought she must be naughty, or, at least, that Agnes thought her so; and after her little heart had been some time swelling with emotion, she at length burst out into tears, saying at the same time, with great vehemence:

'Indeed, Cousin Agnes, I am not naughty!'

'No, you only pretend to be naughty,' said Agnes. 'There, be a good child, and go in the corner, and pretend to be naughty once more, and presently, when you have done crying, I shall come and ask you if you are good.'

'But, indeed, I am good now!' exclaimed Augusta, resisting Agnes as she tried to lead her back to the corner. And I don't like to be naughty! I like to be good!'

'Let me be naughty; it is my turn to be naughty now, Agnes,' said Laura, stepping forwards and taking Augusta's other hand.

'Oh, but it is not half so much fun for you to be naughty,' said Agnes; 'you are such a great girl. Besides, Augusta pretends to cry so well.'

'I don't pretend to cry, and I will not be naughty any more!' said Augusta, who was now irritated into a violent pet; and as she struggled against her cousin, who attempted to draw her to the corner, the poor child was thrown down, and her head hit against the sharp corner of the shell-box.

She gave a loud scream, and Mrs. Clavering and Mrs. Parker hastened to the room. Laura picked up her little sister, on whose forehead there was a severe bruise. Agnes looked pale and ashamed, but no one explained how the accident had happened.

Mrs. Clavering caught up the sobbing Augusta and rang the bell for cold water. The child ran to her mother, who drew aside the curls which almost hid the bruise, and kissing her cheek and forehead, good humouredly assured Mrs. Clavering that it was only a trifling hurt, and in a few minutes tranquillity was restored. But Augusta, whose temper had been more hurt than her forehead, begged that she might accompany her mother to the drawing-room; and as the tea was now nearly ready, Mrs. Clavering told Agnes she might as well bring both of her cousins with her. This arrangement was not very pleasing to Agnes, for she had gained a half-promise from her mother in the morning that she should herself make tea for her cousins in a set of beautiful china which she had lately received from Nottinghamshire; but Mrs. Clavering saw from Augusta's manner of clinging to her mother that something of disagreement had taken place amongst the children, and as she was aware of Agnes's inclination to be the mistress of the party, she judged that it would be better for this evening that the elder and younger parts of the family should make but one party. Agnes was disappointed—very much disappointed; but she fortunately recollected that the disappointment was owing to her own exertion of authority over the poor little Augusta, and she was wise enough to submit in silence. Mrs. Parker, who was always lively and agreeable, brought forward a great many laughable stories for the amusement of the young party; and the mortification of the young tea-maker, and the pain of Augusta's forehead, and, more than this, her anger against her cousin, had all subsided before the urn had done hissing and a pile of plum cakes had been consumed.

This and a great many more days had passed before Agnes paid another visit to her purse, which lay snugly in her mothers' drawer. Neither had her mother's drawer been opened, for Mrs. Clavering had caught a severe cold, and for several days she kept her bed. During this time Agnes was very dull, for although she spent one whole day with her cousins, and another with the little Montagues, there was a great deal of time she was by herself, and being a very sociable little girl, she never preferred being without a companion. Her aunt Parker invited her to come and stay with her entirely during her mother's illness, but Mrs. Clavering preferred her remaining at home. It was fortunate that she did so, for Laura and Augusta Parker a few days after fell severely ill with an infectious fever, and, of course, it was no longer right that they should be visited by their cousin. They were for some days dangerously ill, and when they did begin to get better, it was very slowly, and some weeks passed before it was thought fit that the cousins should meet. It was also some time before Mrs. Clavering was sufficiently recovered to leave the house again, either on foot or in the carriage; but Mrs. Montague frequently called for Agnes, and gave her a ride in her carriage, and after her own way was very kind to her. But her way was that of indulging her, as she did her own children, in every wish they expressed. Whatever toys or trinkets they wished for were purchased for them, and so unreasonable had they been in their wishes that Mrs. Montague had at length been driven to refuse their going to the Bazaar altogether; for when there she had not the resolution, as she ought to have had, to deny them any particular thing they had set their minds on. For this reason, they had not been for some time to this tempting repository of pretty things; but, finding that their young friend Agnes was wishing to go thither to purchase a blue bag, they engaged their mother to take them once more, and a day was fixed on for the proposed treat.

Mrs. Clavering was sufficiently recovered to be sitting on the sofa in the drawing-room when Agnes came to petition for her purse.

'And you have settled everything that you are to buy, have you not, my little girl?' said Mrs. Clavering, as she took from the drawer the silken purse and placed it in the hand of the eager Agnes.

'Oh yes, mother,' replied Agnes, scarcely allowing herself time to draw on her gloves, so anxious was she to be going, and she ran towards the door.

'But Mrs. Montague is not come yet, Agnes,' said Mrs. Clavering.

'Oh, I forgot,' replied Agnes, returning towards her mother. Then, telling upon her fingers she went on: 'Blue bag, thimble, needle-book, scissors, winders.'

'And pincushion,' said Mrs. Clavering.

'Oh yes, pincushion; I had forgotten pincushion. Yes, there must be a pincushion.'

'Now, could not you make the pincushion yourself, Agnes?' asked Mrs. Clavering. 'And the needle-case, I should think, too; and Laura would like them better for your making them.'

'I do not think I should be able to make them well enough, mother,' replied Agnes; 'and I should not like to give anything clumsy to Laura. No, I think I shall buy them.'

'Well, do as you please about this,' replied Mrs. Clavering; and Mrs. Montague's carriage being now heard to rattle down to the door, she gave her little girl a hasty kiss, and Agnes ran downstairs and was very soon on her road to the Bazaar.

As they drove through the streets the little Montagues were very eager in describing a beautiful new stall which had been opened since they had been to the Bazaar. It was one of French toys and trinkets, and there were a great many very pretty and very ingenious things exhibiting there. There were dolls, and workboxes, and wire-dancers, and puzzles of every description. And so very anxious were all three of the little girls to see and admire what all the little and great girls, too, of their acquaintance thought so very well worth seeing and admiring that, when they had left the carriage and entered the room, Mrs. Montague could scarcely keep pace with the nimble-footed little party. They paced round and round the lower room, and were just ascending into the upper, when the first thought of the blue bag crossed the recollection of Agnes.

'Oh, my little blue bag!' she said to her young companions; and slipping behind them, stopped at the stall where she had before seen it displayed.

It was sold. This was not the fault of Agnes.

Should they make another for the young lady? It would be ready by to-morrow, and it should be sent home to any place she should appoint.

'Yes—no.'

Agnes was in a great hurry to go upstairs to the French stall, and Harriet and Eliza were both urging her to make haste.

'There will be prettier bags at the French stall, love, most likely,' whispered Mrs. Montague; 'and, if not, you could give this order as you returned downstairs.'

Agnes wanted very little persuasion to despatch her business below, and the three little girls again quickened their pace towards the upstair room.

'How pretty!' 'How beautiful!' 'How curious!' 'Agnes look here,' and 'Harriet see this'; and 'Eliza, pray look at that'; and 'Mother, may I buy this?' and 'Mother, may I buy that?' were the hasty and rapid exclamations of the first few minutes after the young party had arrived at the famed French stall; and so very much inclined were all of them to touch as well as look at everything that the chattering lady behind the counter was at length obliged in the most civil and polite manner to beg that they would be careful, and not touch what they did not want to buy.

But they wanted to buy everything, and found it very difficult to determine what they wanted to buy most; and whatever Harriet and Eliza fixed upon for themselves, Agnes thought that she should like the same for herself. There was no blue bag at this stall, or, if there was, Agnes saw none, nor any other bag. Her attention was first drawn to a droll little fellow upon wires who tumbled over and over again as fast as the eye could follow him. Harriet bought one of these, and Agnes longed for one. By the side of the famous little tumbler there was a glittering row of bright shining scissors, and a thought of Laura glanced across our little Agnes. But the bag was not yet bought. Besides, the bag might be given without the scissors, and the woman said there were but two of these little tumblers ever made. Harriet had purchased the other, and while Laura and the scissors made Agnes for a moment hesitate, a gentleman put his hand upon the remaining tumbler. Agnes looked up eagerly in his face, and then at the woman; and the woman said she believed the young lady was going to buy that. The chance of losing it determined the young lady's wavering resolution, and the tumbler was paid for, and the scissors forgotten. Then came other things equally charming and equally attractive. Laura was again thought of in conjunction with a box of splendid thimbles, a tray of ivory winders, and pincushions, and needle-cases without number. But she could make the pincushion and needle-case, as her mother had advised her, and her mother, no doubt, would give her silk for the purpose; and she could make a thread-case on to the pincushion; and then she should not want any winders. And the thimble, and the scissors? Agnes found it rather difficult to reason away these, but the sudden recollection that her father would be home before New

Year's Day, and that he would assist her in purchasing what she herself could not afford to buy, turned the scale against poor Laura; and at length all the whole list of useful articles designed for the New Year's gift were by degrees abandoned for a collection of showy but childish toys, which were to amuse their possessor a day, but not longer, and perhaps not so long.

Agnes felt ashamed, and hastened on, for her purse was empty.

On returning downstairs the party again passed the stall where the blue bag had first attracted Agnes's admiration on a former visit. The woman who was keeping the stall curtseyed civilly, and asked if she might be allowed to make another bag. Agnes felt ashamed, and hastened on, for her purse was empty. But the feeling did not continue painful very long, for the little party were all in high spirits, and when they were reseated in the carriage, their tongues went fast, and their merriment continued till they arrived at Mrs. Clavering's. The carriage stopped, the step was let down, and Agnes, scarcely allowing herself time to say good-bye to her companions or thank Mrs. Montague for her morning's pleasure, ran upstairs and into the drawing-room to show her treasures to her mother.

'Oh, mother!' said the eager child, as she flew across the room, and began to exhibit the contents of all her little packets, 'did you ever see anything so droll as this pretty fellow?' And the tumbler was placed upon the table. 'And I am sure I never saw anything half so curious as this!' And another paper packet was unrolled.

'And how hot you are, my poor child!' said Mrs. Clavering, thinking of nothing for the first few moments but the heated countenance of her child, and her tippet, which was hanging half off, and her bonnet, which was crushed into any shape but its own. 'Why, what have you been doing with yourself?'

'Only playing with Harriet and Eliza in the carriage,' replied the breathless child, at the same time shrugging her shoulders, for now that the game of romps was over she was beginning to feel rather uncomfortable. 'And look at this very small wee wee humming-top!' And another paper was unrolled. 'And did you ever see such beautiful sweetmeats?' as the fourth and last packet was displayed.

'Well, and where did you get all these things?' said Mrs. Clavering, as she turned from the heated child to the treasures displayed before her.

'Oh, at the Bazaar! There is such a beautiful new stall there, and it is covered with such pretty things!'

'And do you think that Laura will like these things so well as the blue bag, and the rest of the things you talked of buying for her? And do you think they will be as useful to her?'

'Oh, mother,' began stammering Agnes, 'these things—mother—are not—these are not for Laura, mother. These are—these are for myself.'

'Oh, Agnes,' said Mrs. Clavering very gravely, 'you have not been spending all your money upon yourself and these foolish trifles, and forgetting your kind, good-natured cousin Laura?'

Agnes's fingers were now engaged in twisting round and round them the cotton from the reel lying on her mother's lap, and she felt and looked very foolish. For a few moments nothing more was said, but presently Agnes approached closer to her mother and leaned against her.

Mrs. Clavering took no notice of her little girl, and did not, as usual, encourage her endearing advances. Presently Agnes ventured to say:

'It was my own money, mother, and you said I might do as I pleased with it.'

However, Agnes knew a great deal better than to think for a moment that this was any excuse for her selfishness.

'Yes it *was* your own money,' replied Mrs. Clavering, 'and it certainly was given you to spend as you liked. But I am sorry, very sorry, that I have a little girl who never considers anybody's pleasure and amusement but her own.'

'The blue bag was sold,' said Agnes, after a pause of a few minutes, during which she had been picking the pins out of her mother's pincushion and dropping them one by one on the floor.

Mrs. Clavering took the pincushion gently from the hand of her little girl, and desired her to pick up the pins which she had been so carelessly scattering.

'And were all the scissors and pincushions and thimbles sold, too?' continued Mrs. Clavering. 'And would it not have been possible to have had another bag made, like the one you saw the other day?'

'Yes, mother,' replied Agnes, as she replaced the last pin in the pincushion; 'the woman *did* offer to make another, but I had no money left then.'

'This will never do, Agnes, indeed,' said Mrs. Clavering. 'If you are allowed to indulge all your wishes in this way while you continue a child, you will grow up to be a disagreeable and overbearing woman. Did you never read, "Whatsoever ye would that men should do unto you, do ye even so to them"? Come, tell me; try and recollect.' And as Mrs. Clavering spoke her voice softened, and she laid her cheek on the head of her little girl, who had seated herself on a stool at her feet. 'Did you ever read of this?'

'Yes, mother, I have read it in the Bible,' replied Agnes, as she turned round towards her mother, and laid her head coaxingly on her lap.

'It was one of the directions of our blessed Saviour,' continued Mrs. Clavering, 'and His directions we ought always to obey. Now, supposing that your Cousin Laura had determined to give you anything she knew you were very desirous of having, should you like her to change her mind, because she fancied something for herself which she could not purchase without doing so? Should you not think she was unkind in doing so?'

'Yes, mother,' replied Agnes; 'but Laura did not know I was going to give it her, and therefore she will not think me unkind.'

'No, but you will know that you have been so,' replied Mrs. Clavering; 'and I know that you have been so, and I am very much hurt that you are so, for, as I have frequently told you, I do not like such little selfish ways as you too frequently indulge.'

Agnes did not feel comfortable, and she had not half the enjoyment of her new purchases which she expected to have; and she had very little pleasure in showing them to her cousins, who were allowed on the next day, for the first time since their illness, to come and play with her. The tumbler was not half so droll as he seemed to be before she bought him. Augusta, however, was delighted with him. She laughed aloud at all his whimsical changes, and Agnes told her that she might have it if she liked for she was tired of it—not a very disinterested reason, but Augusta was pleased with her present, and also with the sweetmeats of which she partook, and some of which she carried home to her brothers who were never forgotten.

New Year's Day was now approaching very fast, and as it did approach Agnes thought a great deal of the little blue bag, and she longed for her father's return, for she thought that he would give her money if she asked for it, and still the present might be made. But New Year's Day arrived, and no father. Mr. Clavering had been detained by business, and might not be at home yet for some weeks. Poor Agnes! her last hope gone. An invitation to dinner arrived from Uncle and Aunt Parker. It was Laura's birthday, and the two families generally on that day had dined together.

On the day before Agnes felt very serious for some minutes together, and when the thoughts of the blue bag crossed her, none of her play-things amused her, and she was grave, and very near shedding tears several times. Mrs. Clavering watched these emotions in her little girl, but took no notice of them till the following morning, when, calling her to her side, she said:

'Agnes, I think you feel very sorry that you have been so selfish, and I am sure that you have not enjoyed yourself half so much with the variety of different things you have bought for your own gratification as you would have done if you had persevered in spending your money, according to your first intentions, on your cousin Laura. Now, I do not like that Laura should lose her present, nor do I wish that you should suffer any more mortification than you have done for the fault you have committed, so that I have been endeavouring to make an arrangement for you that shall enable you still to oblige your cousin. You remember asking me a day or two since why I did not purchase new chimney ornaments, for that mine looked very shabby? It was my intention to have done so yesterday, for you know that I have pleasure in seeing the mantelpiece prettily ornamented, particularly as your father is always kind enough to admire it when it is so. But I have given up this intention at present that I might use the money which would have been required for the purpose in a different way; and if, my dearest child,' continued the affectionate mother, as a tear started into her eye, 'I can teach you by this, or by any other means, to learn to sacrifice your own desires to those of others, I shall never regret that the money has been employed in the purchase of a little blue bag.'

Thus saying, Mrs. Clavering opened the drawer of her work-table, and exhibited a bag, the exact copy of the one which Agnes had first fixed on as a New Year's gift for her cousin. It was as completely furnished within as it was elegant on the outside. There was the gold thimble, the gold sheath to the scissors, the tortoiseshell needle-case, the ivory winders, and the pincushion edged with blue, and stuck in minikin pins, with the words, 'Affection—from Agnes to Laura,' Agnes's little heart swelled with emotion. She threw her arms round the neck of her mother, and sobbed aloud, as she promised never again to be a selfish little girl.

Agnes threw her arms round the neck of her dear Laura.

'Your feelings now, my sweet girl, are strongly excited,' said Mrs. Clavering, as she pressed the lovely child in her arms, 'and at this moment I know you mean to perform all that you promise. You will find it difficult, perhaps, to keep your promise; but you must strive hard to do so, and in time no doubt you will succeed. Now go and get your pelisse and bonnet put on, for the carriage will soon be at the door.'

Agnes tripped away with light steps and a merrier heart than she expected would be her companion to her uncle's. The carriage was shortly after ready, and the cousins in half an hour were together. Oh, how grateful did Agnes feel to her mother when Laura met her! In Laura's arms was the box of shells which she had received from her uncle abroad, and which was now quite full; for Laura had denied herself everything that she might complete the collection, and she now presented it, with a feeling of calm and quiet pleasure, to her beloved cousin. Agnes felt ashamed and pleased, humbled and gratified, as she threw her arms round the neck of her dear Laura to thank her, and as she presented to the delighted girl, in return for her beautiful box of shells, the thimble, the scissors, the needle-case, the winders, the pincushion, and the little blue bag.

Lector House believes that a society develops through a two-fold approach of continuous learning and adaptation, which is derived from the study of classic literary works spread across the historic timeline of literature records. Therefore, we aim at reviving, repairing and redeveloping all those inaccessible or damaged but historically as well as culturally important literature across subjects so that the future generations may have an opportunity to study and learn from past works to embark upon a journey of creating a better future.

This book is a result of an effort made by Lector House towards making a contribution to the preservation and repair of original ancient works which might hold historical significance to the approach of continuous learning across subjects.

HAPPY READING & LEARNING!

LECTOR HOUSE LLP
E-MAIL: lectorpublishing@gmail.com